RAZE VS THE HUNT

Raze vs The Hunt

Book two in the Raze Warfare series

SHELLEY CASS

For those who are a work in progress.
For those who are willing to be Raze in their own way.
For those who know that love is love, and how greatly the world
needs it.

A trigger warning for readers: there are
confronting drug and violence scenes in this novel.

RECEIVE YOUR EXTRA RAZE WARFARE CHAPTER WHEN YOU SIGN UP FOR SHELLEY CASS' VIP LIST. GET YOUR BONUS HERE:

shelleycass.com/coming-soon-02

LINK TO FREE VIP READER GIFT

Razes, Razes fight the dark.
Razes, Razes, are the mark …

| 1 |

One

The bar lights were dim, but Kiddo could see everything.

The gorgeous young woman leaned across Dom to pour him another saké. She tilted so far into him that she was leaning her free hand on the wooden bench between his legs – forcing his knees to go wide.

Kiddo tried to stare past the two of them. At the dark red tones of the wall behind them.

His leg was jumping in agitation.

She crooned something to Dom in Japanese, pressing the glass to his lips. Kiddo could infer that it was something along the lines of: "I've sure missed you, sexy."

Kiddo squinted at the soft, golden lantern lights around the room. The Japanese characters painted down long wall banners. The giant masterpiece of inky ocean art – crashing, blue waves that were taking up an entire wall behind the crowded bar.

Tipsy, the young woman returned the glass to the table, and then leaned a little too far into Dom, laughing softly as she half fell into his lap. He snaked a hand up her spine to support the back of her neck, tilting her head so that she was gazing up at him.

Her long ponytail swept to the side in a shining, jet-black stream, tickling over Dom's fingers. Her hair was as glossy and slippery as the short, black satin slip that she wore. That he was touching.

"In English, remember Blossom?" Dom told her silkily.

Kiddo blew upward at his fringe, crossing his arms and bouncing his other leg now too.

"My pretty Raze," the young woman pouted. "I am just so glad to have you here again. My mistress has pined for you."

"She might be unhappy that you haven't told her of my arrival yet," Dom smiled.

"But you've hardly been here a minute," Blossom answered, straightening, yet as close up against Dom as she could manage, so that he draped his arm around her slender shoulders.

"These saké bomb glasses, and the empty jug say otherwise," Dom replied, stroking the black river of her hair.

"I haven't even started us on my Hot Shots," she protested flirtatiously.

Kiddo tried to focus on a woman entertaining a large table across the room. Her dark hair was combed up elaborately, her kimono had a flower print, her lips were a startling red against the white paint on her face, and she played some kind of string instrument. Everyone was mesmerised by her – and she might have even been a real geisha – but all Kiddo could hear was Blossom murmuring sweet nothings.

"You know, you have possibly become even *more* beautiful." She traced Dom's jawline.

"That is the appearance of contentment," Dom supplied.

"Muri. *No.* Content? Without me?" she gasped playfully, lightly slapping at his chest.

Kiddo rolled his eyes.

"Maybe you should get a room," he muttered before he could stop himself. But realised that the idea of them doing that was much worse.

Dom had heard it. The corner of his lip quirked up. He re-filled Blossom's glass, and she did the same for him.

"Your companion is also quite spectacular," Blossom commented, not hurt at all. "Who is he to you?"

"My contentment," Dom answered, flicking wicked eyes in Kiddo's direction so that Kiddo slumped down under the scrutiny.

Blossom drew Dom's attention back, putting her fingertips under his chin and pressing her lips to his.

The hot, tense chemistry was palpable. Kiddo felt like the whole bar wasn't watching the scene in suspense, holding their breaths and near passing out, until Blossom finally released Dom.

"Are you two going steady?" she purred. As if that entire stretch of time hadn't just passed.

Dom was watching Kiddo again, his lips curling. "We've never defined it."

Kiddo glared.

"Perhaps we'll define it after this," Dom amended thoughtfully.

"You've never been the sort," Blossom exclaimed, reclining in his arms. "He must be special."

"Oh he is."

Blossom ran her fingers through Dom's hair, raking it back so that he became more than ever like a modern greaser heartthrob.

Kiddo had gauged, in the very short time that he'd been here, that everyone else in Japan seemed *way* less touchy. Why did Dom have to attract the touchiest people?

"Raaaze?"

The word was almost whispered, as if the name had caused a moment of prolonged, heart stopping longing for the man who had uttered it.

"Great," Kiddo grumbled.

A tall Japanese man, youthful and lithe, was now standing over their table, over Dom, regarding him with wide eyes.

"Ryo," Dom grinned.

"It is so good to see you." The young man reached forward to clasp the back of Dom's neck, squeezing the base of Dom's skull lovingly. "Why didn't you come straight down? You know you don't need an invitation to see her."

Blossom sat up straighter then. "Yes, since when do you use the main entrance?" she questioned. "As nice as it has been to catch up."

"Since maybe we wanted a drink," Dom shrugged.

Blossom narrowed her eyes. "Your friend hasn't touched a drop." Then her pierced brow lifted and she stared at Dom in delighted accusation. "You used me."

Kiddo frowned.

"You wanted to be noticed," Blossom added.

"With Blossom's help, and now my reaction," Ryo mused seriously, "you will have been noticed. There are people here who will know Raze is one of our favourites."

Dom lifted one shoulder and dropped it. "I don't mind if word gets out that the original Raze is here. And I don't mind paying the price for the affections of your master. Or for the affections of her two lovely apprentices."

Kiddo felt some of his surliness dissolve. He almost regretted the daggers he'd been glaring into Blossom.

Almost.

"Something interesting must be happening for you to be making your presence known," Ryo stated. "So I think it's time Blossom gets back to work up here, and I take you down to the part of mistress' domain that you are most used to."

Blossom kissed Dom's cheekbone. Then she rose, and gave Dom a slight, informal bow.

Kiddo much preferred that style of interaction.

"This place won't guard itself," she sighed, flicking her hair and leaving.

Kiddo blinked. She was drunk. She had been sitting on Dom for ages. She was in *charge*? And in charge of guarding the entrance?

"Believe it or not, her reputation alone stops many people from trying anything here," Ryo told Kiddo, catching his expression. "She is fierce."

"You have both been trained by the best," Dom agreed, rising now himself. "This is Kiddo."

"Hazimemashite. I am Ryo," the young man bowed his

head in greeting to Kiddo. "This is the first time Raze has brought a friend into our midst," he said, as they followed him through the crowd and toward a corridor past the kitchens.

"You make me sound like such a loner," Dom commented breezily.

"You are," Ryo agreed. "But I am pleased that you have found someone you trust so closely to let into your world."

"You should be pleased that I trust you well enough to introduce you to someone in my world," Dom smiled.

Ryo chuckled, a little wistfully. "I've seen every inch of you. I thought I was part of your world myself."

Oh, there was that surliness again.

They traversed a dim hallway, its length adorned with traditional Japanese art. But when they took a right hand corridor, the adornments ended.

Ryo led them toward a door with an official sign that likely read 'staff only.'

"Don't ever go in there," Ryo warned Kiddo light heartedly. "It's a broom cupboard."

"And this one?" Kiddo asked gruffly, gesturing at what did appear to be a broom cupboard.

"A labyrinth that *looks* like it would lead to something important," Ryo told him. "But that is full of traps."

"Clever trickery," Kiddo replied, trying not to seem as grumpy as he felt.

Ryo probably thought he was a churlish, oversized kid, to suit his name.

"This one, on the other hand," Ryo said, gesturing at a

large washing trolley, which was brimming with white sheets and tablecloths. "Is the entrance you are after."

He pressed an apparently random part of the canvas side of the trolley, and there was a faint beep. Then the trolley's side opened like a door.

Instead of white linens spilling out upon the floor, Kiddo saw that the sheets only rested upon a hard platform over a hollow opening. And the canvas walls of the trolley disguised a heavily reinforced entrance, which opened onto a stairway.

"Very clever trickery," Kiddo admitted begrudgingly.

"This is the most direct access you will get to my mistress from the bar," Ryo answered. "Yet it still has its tricks. Do you remember your way?"

"We've got it from here," Dom grinned. "Thank you."

Dom and Kiddo ducked under the low entrance and stepped down onto the staircase.

"Ki o tsukete," Ryo farewelled them, and sealed the door closed.

| 2 |

Two

"You are so terrible at hiding your feelings," Dom told Kiddo happily. "I love it."

"She was all over you. And he was in *love* with you."

"We just haven't seen each other in a while," Dom grinned. The lighting was dim in here too, but Kiddo could make out his mischievous expression.

"He seems to remember seeing every bit of you, in exquisite detail."

Ryo had made the memory seem like a rather sublime one. Something Kiddo could recognise in his own memories of a naked Dom.

"Why didn't you tell me you were being man-candy up there for a reason?"

"Man-candy," Dom sniggered. "Are you less jealous if it was all with a purpose?"

Kiddo glared.

"You were way more jealous when Sparks had a fling," Dom pondered. "Why am I not insulted?"

Kiddo gritted his teeth, remembering Blake. Big lug, newbie *Blake*, leaning Sparks against one of her cars. Their faces drawing close.

Then the surprise on Big ol Blake's face as Kiddo had yanked him backward by the collar.

He'd made an odd 'heuuc' sound as Kiddo had whipped him around, and straight into a row of knuckles.

"I didn't mean to scare him off," Kiddo defended half-heartedly.

That was *exactly* what his lack of impulse control had been up to.

"I thought he was making her uncomfortable."

Dom snorted. Sparks would never tolerate anyone making her uncomfortable.

That had cost the gang a few potential Raze recruits from the flighty snatcher competitors they'd saved. But really, it was important to sort the strong ones from those who couldn't take a little ruffling.

"And anyway, I was just a child. Still in school, adjusting medications, and cracking under exam stress," Kiddo huffed. "I've matured."

"That was last year. And you only just graduated," Dom laughed. "Which I am very proud of, by the way. I misted right up."

"Yes, but Hato outright cried."

Dom chortled. "It's always the big ones who surprise you. I wouldn't have expected that big bulky Blake to cry after one little bop either."

It hadn't really been just a little bop.

Kiddo had felt pretty bad about that particular overreaction, even after Sparks had forgiven him.

"This is different," Kiddo glowered, and jerked Dom aside – pushing him against the corridor wall to force him to stop.

"Now, *how* is it different when it's me?" Dom drawled, unruffled by the fact that he was being held fast.

The liquor had added fire to Dom's eyes. They burned brightly, glittering with keen energy.

Dom leaned forward to whisper beside Kiddo's ear. Making him shiver. "This is pretty hot by the way."

Kiddo remembered another time, when Dom had been the one to throw Kiddo up against a wall in a hidden, underground corridor.

It was becoming a habit.

Kiddo bit his lip and pulled back to gaze at Dom.

"You and I never did define our unorthodox relationship," Dom smouldered. "In fact, that's something Sparks likes best about the three of us."

It was one reason Kiddo was so apologetic for spoiling something Sparks might have wanted to start with someone else. He hadn't wanted to push her away from what they shared with her.

"Well … yes," Kiddo answered. "That works for the three of us."

He leaned on, more than imprisoned Dom now.

"Mmm?"

"But," Kiddo furrowed his brow. "Maybe not for the two of us."

Kiddo felt his stomach and heart jump with the effort it had taken to spit that out.

"*Finally,*" Dom uttered, evilly. The alcohol danced on the breath issued with that word.

"I never said anything because you didn't think you were capable of being conventional," Kiddo frowned.

"And *I* never pushed because of your past," Dom explained almost gently. "I thought you might not handle being pinned down by commitment."

"Not when it comes to you," Kiddo confessed earnestly. "I don't mind being pinned down by you."

"Me neither, evidently." Dom smirked down lazily at Kiddo's grip on him. "I might be a flirt, and I might love the family of three we've got going on. But Sparks is happy doing her own thing. She'll join us as she pleases. You, on the other hand, are my always."

Kiddo felt heat touch his cheeks and the tips of his ears. "And, am I also your *only*?"

He winced even as he said it. So corny. But he had to know.

Dom tilted his head. "Apart from Sparks. And the flirting – which is always innocent, and generally has a goal by the way. You are the only 'only' I've ever had or wanted."

"So ..." Kiddo swallowed.

Dom's gaze was unwavering. "You're mine, and I'm yours. Officially."

Kiddo nodded, awash with relief, and he felt Dom's hands come up to settle on his sides.

"We've been that way from the start really," Dom said. "And now I am bringing you into another part of my life."

Kiddo nodded again, shorter and sharper. "You're right. We're meant to be doing something important here."

"Yes, we are," Dom acknowledged. "But that was important too."

Kid lingered, and Dom didn't move his hands from where they held Kiddo either.

Finally, Kiddo couldn't help it. He broke into a smile, and tugged on Dom's jacket to pull him into a kiss.

It didn't even matter, that much, that Dom tasted of cherry blossom lip gloss as well as the saké.

He was Dom's, and Dom was his.

"Alright," Kiddo said after a moment. "Lead on."

| 3 |

Three

There was a left hand turn, an oddly placed fire exit, and a ladder down into a system of massive concrete tunnels.

"This isn't going to flood with sewerage is it?" Kiddo asked, his voice echoing. Though they didn't seem like the kinds of ominous, underground channels for sludge one would expect. The passageways were surprisingly clean, open and bright, with white light strips illuminating the way.

"These are actually privately owned, off the records types of tunnels," Dom answered. "But they do connect to all kinds of unappealing piping systems that can help you pop up all over Tokyo."

"Gross. But convenient," Kiddo admitted.

"Not quite as cosy as our dock-side tunnel back at base," Dom sighed. "But they'll do."

They entered a wide tunnel with more traffic in it. People were moving about into other large pipes, or milling in groups and talking. A few people eyed Dom distrustfully. Some just warily, or others with interest. A number nodded their heads in greeting and recognition.

It was a mixed bunch.

Some wore business attire, others wore high brand fashion apparel, then there were the ones who had the rough look of the streets – the ones with the piercings, studs, rips and zips. They were the friendlier ones.

"Why are they watching you like that?" Kiddo asked in a low voice.

"Oh," Dom waved it off. "The ones gazing with open adoration and welcome? I might have worked with some or saved others from snatchers."

"And the other ones?" The less enthused ones.

"They just don't know me!" Dom waved that off too. "It's hard to trust an outsider with such a close connection to the top, when you're a hierarchy kind of person," he shrugged. "Or maybe they just aren't smiley people."

They crossed into another connecting tunnel, but this one was painted jade green. Along the rounded walls, fairy lights hung in life-sized, ornamental blossom trees made out of pink and white crystals.

"Except that guy. That guy definitely dislikes me," Dom hissed out of the corner of his mouth as they passed a sour, middle aged man with a totally bald head. "I might have upset him and his business partners at a dinner a couple of years back."

The man had stopped his sweeping, directing a snarl Dom's way.

"What did you do?" Kiddo asked curiously.

Dom smiled over his shoulder at the bald man still glaring after them, and gripping his broom rather hard.

"I let the master of this house know that mister baldie had

started to deal with snatchers," Dom answered. "It was quite a public announcement, at quite the lovely dinner, and among a highly anti-snatcher audience. But I waited until they had given us all first drinks and finger foods."

"You're both still in one piece …" Kiddo remarked.

The bald man's sweeping finally resumed.

"Oh, he's missing an important one now," Dom answered. "And he's paying for his mistake by living down here permanently in servitude. They give *him* all the jobs that require someone to run through those sewerage tunnels we were talking about, and he can't step foot in the best part of this underworld kingdom."

"And his business partners?"

"Lost a very wealthy connection, and now treat him like a leper," Dom said smugly. "He no longer has a name. Stripped of everything. Now wait until you see this next bit!"

A guard in a red, wide sleeved robe, tied at the waist, bowed slightly to Dom and waved him on.

They reached the end of the jade green tunnel, and Kiddo halted in surprise.

It opened up to a cavern so large that a small Japanese village, a wide man-made lagoon, manicured gardens, and a traditional house in the centre – styled much like a miniature shogun palace – all fit into the space easily.

"Wow..." Kiddo uttered flatly.

"Yup," Dom grinned. He tugged Kiddo to follow him down a pebbled path.

Different tunnel openings were spotted about the cavern,

visible in the distance with red robed figures on guard. And greenhouse lights lit the whole scene up like day.

Both the smaller, wooden houses, as well as the main, palace styled house sported roofs with jade tiles and golden dragon statues. They were surrounded by elevated verandas, and crystal blossom trees decorated each garden.

"This is the most outside feeling inside place I've ever been to," Kiddo managed. He noticed koi fish among the lily pads of the lagoon as Dom led Kiddo over a bridge, heading toward the intimate village now.

The scents of fresh earth, flowers, raw wood and incense made Kiddo feel more relaxed at once.

"This was my house," Dom gestured at a traditional cottage casually. It would only have been made up of a couple of rooms, but it was lovely.

Kiddo guffawed, doing a double take and halting.

"You were given a *house*? And you left *this* to come and slither through our air conditioning chutes at base?"

"Pretty sure I still have a nice abode in India too," Dom remarked thoughtfully. "And, surprisingly, your air conditioning chutes weren't that dusty."

Kiddo's mouth opened, and some strangled sounds made their way out, but that was about it.

"Oh come now," Dom chided. "This house was a thank you and mark of welcome. But I couldn't stay safely down here in this den and still be Raze. I needed to be closer to the action." He resumed his tour, pointing out each spot. "These are the houses of our great lady's male consorts, closest guards, maids, and her apprentices – Blossom and Ryo."

"And *this*," came a withering voice, deep and charismatic, "is where a more dutiful brat would have come to pay his respects immediately."

Kiddo and Dom were within sight of the main house.

The sliding door was open, and in the main chamber there sat a formidable woman. She was round and broad, with tough features. And she was giving Dom her most cutting expression. An expression that indeed gave the impression that it could actually, truly cut.

"Brat?" Dom asked; wounded.

Cut to kill.

"Oh alright," Dom smiled his devastatingly winsome smile, and brought Kiddo up the cultivated path and veranda steps.

He paused to give the magnetic woman a truly respectful bow, which Kiddo sought to mirror, before they removed their shoes and stepped down into her abode.

"Zetsumyōna," the woman stated flatly, her sharp eyes roving from Dom to Kiddo, and lingering there.

"Miss Lotus," Dom said, in possibly the politest tone Kiddo had ever heard him use. "This is Kiddo Lake."

Miss Lotus gave a curt nod, and gestured for them to join her on a large straw mat, where she sat regally amongst an array of cushions.

"She called you exquisite," Dom told Kiddo encouragingly, as they seated themselves on the softly woven rushes, cross legged before her.

Though she was much older and her straight long hair

was startlingly white, her skin was smooth. Her curves made her seem strong and her unbent posture made her seem vital.

Miss Lotus' eyes were framed by sharp, dark liner and flicks of crimson eyeshadow. Her lips and kimono were just as red as the robes of her guards.

She seemed capable of magic. For Kiddo had never felt so still, and even bashful. He sat without fidgeting, and didn't even have to try to keep his gaze from wandering to the intricate scenes painted on screens and hanging art along the walls of the lantern lit space.

"Are you from here?" Miss Lotus asked, evaluating Kiddo in return. Measuring him up. "You're Japanese?"

"I'm not sure, Miss Lotus," Kiddo answered. "I never knew my parents."

She eyed him, taking in his features. "A shame not to know."

A pretty young maid, with crystal blossoms dangling from a fine comb in her hair, brought a tray with a teapot and small jade cups. She set it down, pouring steaming green tea for them, before retreating deferentially.

"You are a fine pair," Miss Lotus decided. "Striking. Though I never thought Raze would find his match."

"And you are breathtaking, of course, too," Dom returned amiably. "Especially with your teeth in."

Miss Lotus snorted delicately. "The Irishman found you, did he?"

"Actually, I found Flip first," Dom answered. "Why'd you try to scare him?"

She assumed a haughty expression. "I don't have to put effort in for just anybody. But I did deem him a worthy enough person in the end, and eventually put my dentures in."

"You must have, for him to have walked back out of here," Dom nodded. "And, you needn't try when it comes to us either. You are glorious."

"*Glorious.*" Her lips curled, the red edges of her smile curving delicately. "I remember how you looked. Stretched out here in these cushions each time I decorated that body. Blossom and Ryo were so charitable in wanting to be here to assist."

Kiddo willed himself to stay Zen.

Zen.

Zen.

Zen.

"Have you brought him back for new additions? There is space on his skin yet." Miss Lotus directed the power of her attention back to Kiddo again. "Or have you brought him back to me to stay? A partner of Raze is welcome to stay too."

"I'm sorry, Miss Lotus," Kiddo replied. "I don't think anyone could ask him to settle in one place."

She clicked her tongue. "True. I have kept your house ready, and it will always be waiting for you. What more can I do?" she asked Dom, rhetorically.

"You have also been an ally in deterring snatchers or taking in vulnerable youths," Dom answered anyway. "And you are someone I can turn to when I need a favour ..."

"Ahh," she scowled. "So there *is* something you want from me."

She picked up a silk fan by her side, flicking it open with

an audible click. Birds with bright feathers were printed across the fan's pleats.

"Spit it out then."

Dom was equally as charming and disarming when he was earnest as when he was behaving rakishly. "We need your help while we go about locating a missing friend."

Miss Lotus softened a little. "One of those friends you left me for good for?" she asked. "The Irishman?"

Kiddo gazed down at his hands, stopping himself from kneading his palms.

"Seethe," Dom answered.

"Ah. One of your first childhood companions," Miss Lotus recalled. "You did not know if he and the other had been ruined by their snatching."

"You've heard of the Raze gang that sprang up in my wake when I left?"

"I have heard of it," Miss Lotus affirmed, fanning herself sedately. "I had half thought you alone were capable of bouncing around the world and taking down five snatcher bases by yourself."

"Six now," Dom informed her. "Without buyer confidence, more will likely follow. But I'm not working alone on this anymore. My old friends, and a growing number of new ones, have joined me."

"Quite the personal development for you," she congratulated him.

"And now quite the personal loss," Dom answered.

Miss Lotus regarded him with a touch of empathy.

"It makes sense that the snatchers would bite back," Miss Lotus told him honestly, her tone still discerning.

"But I want the final bite," Dom said. "I want Seethe back."

"Perhaps you've bitten off more than you can chew." She sipped from her delicate, thimble shaped tea cup. "You've made a lot of enemies."

Dom scowled. "Good," he said flatly. "Only scum hate me."

She nodded slowly, and set her cup down.

Kiddo supposed that was true. Even when Dom had been a suspicious stranger breaking into Hato's to talk to Kiddo each night, Kid had never disliked or even distrusted him. It had been near impossible to.

"So why were you drawing the attention of your enemies, using Blossom to broadcast your arrival?" Miss Lotus asked at last. "And yes," she eyed him matter-of-factly. "Of course I heard about that."

Kiddo raised a sardonic eyebrow at Dom himself.

"I was being a yummy piece of man-candy," Dom said sheepishly, and flicked Kiddo a quick smile before becoming serious again. "Because I think the snatchers took Seethe when they were looking for me instead. I'm hoping they'll keep him alive when they know I'm going to try to get him back. They'll keep him as bait."

"Indeed," Miss Lotus mulled it over.

Kiddo had guessed as much. But it wasn't a great alternative to Seethe being missing.

"Do you think they seek to take revenge on you?" Miss Lotus mused. "Or to stop your Raze movement in its tracks?"

"They mustn't realise that it's so much bigger than me, and always has been," Dom shrugged.

"Why would I let you leave here, knowing that they're

closing in on *my* Raze, of all the Razes that exist now?" Miss Lotus shifted her weight, her long kimono tucked around the rounded shape of her legs.

Kiddo was starting to like the idea of just staying down here with Dom too. To heck with the culinary school he was signed up for after the break. But he couldn't say to heck with Seethe or the others.

"I would pine, I would whine, I would drive you crazy," Dom told her with a grin. "You'd be tossing me out soon yourself anyway."

"Then what," her eyes glittered darkly, "can I do to assist my favourite?"

| 4 |

Four

One of the decorative room dividers had been pulled aside. And at the press of a button, a sleek, wide screen had slid out from a wooden compartment in a wall.

Now Jingle, Hato and Start's faces were filling that screen as Start pitched his plan. It was clear that even these three savvy Razes found Miss Lotus to be quite incredible, despite it being from across the distance.

"Dom is going to need to make himself as un-obviously obvious as possible," Start was saying, licking his lips almost nervously. "So that he can get himself attacked and we can catch ourselves one of the snatchers. Or at least tail them. Ma'am." He tagged the polite term on at the end when he caught sight of how unimpressed Miss Lotus seemed at that idea.

Kiddo would be sticking to Dom like glue.

"We have only a general idea of what area Seethe disappeared from, but we unfortunately can't hone it in enough to find any surveillance of it happening," Start said regretfully, adjusting his glasses. "So we don't know enough about which vehicle to look for, what direction he was taken in, or where his snatchers might be hiding."

Miss Lotus' lips were a thin, red line. "They are brave indeed to be rearing their heads in my area. They had to know I would find out."

"Your reputation alone has kept your area safe in the past," Hato agreed in a low voice. "So the stakes must be high for them to be willing to risk your disfavour, and to take one of the Raze gang in particular."

"What we beg of you, madam," Start went on, "is for your connections to be as vigilant as ever – passing on word to you of possible snatcher sites. Or finding witnesses who might know something. However, we also ask that you keep your people, and the law enforcement, away from what *we* are up to. If we're not careful, we could lose Seethe, and the original Raze."

"We are sending a small team to watch over and work with Dom and Kiddo from a distance," Jingle stated then. It was early morning for them, but she was as bright and sharp as ever, with pink sparkle eyeshadow and a purple tie in her hair. "We are hoping, with your help, that nobody will expose them or make trouble for them."

"Or take them too," Hato added darkly.

Miss Lotus was quiet for a few moments. Considering.

And the gang held their breath.

"Fine," she acquiesced at last. "I will take care of as much as I can."

Start sighed in relief and Jingle smiled broadly.

"Send me their details," Miss Lotus instructed curtly. "For

Raze, I will make sure your team has safe passage." She directed her dark eyes to Dom. "They can stay here. With me."

Kiddo's jaw dropped. Dom had said that only the most important and trusted of Miss Lotus' inner circle could enter this oasis at the centre of the underground. Or temporary esteemed guests, curiosities and prisoners.

She *really* adored him.

Or she counted his gang as esteemed and curious enough to imprison.

"I'll send their information through now." Jingle brought up the identification files of Trix, Pash, Quicklips, Velvet and Tiny.

Sparks would be running her mechanics and weapons business. Hato and Flip would keep overseeing the Raze movement and training of new recruits. And Frazzle was plenty busy setting up the new medical wing that Hato had commissioned. It was nearly finished.

"Send any flight details too," Miss Lotus ordered. "Make sure they sit separately. I'll have people collect and bring them here by various entrances."

"We can hardly express our gratitude," Hato rumbled seriously. He was as powerful as ever, Jingle and Start barely fitting into the screen on either side of his broad frame. But there was a slight downward slant to his shoulders, and a tight expression to his face that gave away his worry.

Seethe was Hato's closest and oldest friend. They had not been separated since childhood, and the moment they had separated for Seethe to take a holiday – he was snatched. It would be like re-living a terrible nightmare.

Kiddo felt his stomach knot at the thought of what it must have been like for Seethe to have been taken again; this time alone, and for Hato now.

When the call ended, Kiddo fidgeted listlessly. Downcast.

"I am so grateful for your friendship," Dom told Miss Lotus. "You are very generous."

Miss Lotus coolly lifted a thin, painted eyebrow. "I am the gift that keeps on giving. Go to your minka to rest. You will find a hot bath, a lit hearth and ramen waiting for you."

She flicked her fingers at him, palm down in a shoo of dismissal.

"I worship you, magnificent mistress," Dom fawned over her, taking her hand mid shooing motion and bowing over it as Kiddo rose.

Kiddo did feel bone tired.

Hato had announced that he'd received word about Seethe having been snatched just that morning. Dom had been the closest in the world to, and most familiar with Japan. And Kiddo was on break, so he had packed a bag at once to go to meet Dom while the others organised and worked out a plan of action.

Kiddo had met Dom at Tokyo's Narita airport that evening, and they had caught a train straight to Lotus Bar.

"Oh, heaven," Dom uttered as he eased the cottage's door open, and the cleansing, musky smell of incense rolled out over them.

While they had talked with Miss Lotus, the great cavern's greenhouse lights had lowered substantially, and fires and fairy lights had been lit around the grounds.

The glowing lanterns and hearth inside the small cottage,

along with the low table set with steaming noodles in bowls, made this cosy space into the most inviting place in the world.

"I am so lucky you did decide to give this all up," Kiddo told Dom, staring at the noodle broth hungrily and with interest – taking note of the thin meat slices, herbs, egg and various ingredients he might try to emulate in future.

"There's so much I'd be missing if I hadn't," Dom answered, slapping Kid on the butt before sinking down at the table. "Now hurry up and join me. It's our first meal as a couple. And that was our first couple's butt slap too, come to think of it."

Kiddo smiled, and took his spot on a cushion beside Dom.

| 5 |

Five

They had noticed that their bags had been placed neatly inside the doorway. Blossom or Ryo must have sent them down from the bar.

Then, full of noodles and broth, Dom had insisted they get into the bath.

Their 'first bath as a couple'.

He was sprawled out, laying back against Kiddo, with one leg over the side of the tub, humming cheerfully as he cupped water in a hand and let it waterfall back down.

Kiddo was running a bar of soap over the angriest of dragons glaring out from Dom's pectoral muscles. And Kiddo didn't even consider answering the incoming video call he noticed flashing from his phone screen on the basin.

Dom, on the other hand, didn't hesitate to dry his hand and reach for his own phone when he heard it vibrating against the wooden floor.

"Don't you dare," Kiddo warned when Dom moved to accept the insistent call from Hato. "It'll be our first argument as a couple."

Dom chuckled. Pressing the option to join without the camera on.

Hato appeared, with Jingle beside him again, and Hato frowned into his lens.

"Why can't I see you?" Hato asked in low consternation. "Did I press something wrong?"

"You didn't press anything wrong," Jingle assured him briskly. "Why are you hiding?" she asked Dom.

Kiddo held his breath.

"I'm on the toilet," Dom snickered.

His voice did echo through the small washroom in a questionable way.

"Uh," Hato grimaced. "We'll call back."

"No, no," Dom sighed. "I'm in for the long haul, I'm afraid."

Kiddo tried not to laugh despite himself.

"We'll try Kid again," Jingle suggested.

That stopped Kiddo's chuckles.

"Mmm, he's also on the toilet," Dom lied.

Kiddo pinched Dom so that he yelped and wriggled, sloshing the water.

"I mean, in bed. After going to the toilet, he went to bed."

"What's that sloshing?" Jingle asked in distaste. "And why did you squeal? What in the world did you both eat?"

"I have not ever squealed in my life," Dom told her archly, flicking at the water's surface with disdain. "Sometimes a man simply needs to express himself in the privy."

"Is Kiddo alright?" Hato moved his face closer to the screen, as if it would help him to see something on their end.

"We are both *fine*," Dom grinned. "You saw us hardly half an hour ago, but it's late here. What have you got to tell us? Me, I mean. I'll pass it on to Kiddo. When I'm no longer alone. On the john."

Hato glared over his shoulder at where Flip had just wandered into view. He'd opened the fridge and was uncapping the lid of the milk.

"Glass," Hato told him.

Flip sighed and wandered back out of view, making clinking sounds in the glass cupboard. Then there was the shuffling sound of a cereal packet opening as Flip went about breakfast.

Kiddo hated to think of the pile of dishes that would be starting to grow already.

"We're calling because we thought it was worth mentioning that the snatchers must have caught word of your, or the real Raze's Japanese connections," Jingle announced.

"They might have been in wait for you, and just jumped at the first of the Raze gang to appear in Tokyo," Hato elaborated. "And it might have even been someone associated with Miss Lotus who told them that Raze might go to Tokyo at all."

Kiddo dropped the bar of soap and it sploshed noisily before clunking audibly against the bottom of the tub.

"Ew, gross," Jingle groaned.

"Apologies," Dom tried not to laugh. "I still think having Miss Lotus' protection will mean there are more people for than against us. I think even if there are a few rotten apples down here, it's safer to stay with her, and to utilise the many secret ways of getting here as a protected, guarded base, than to go it alone."

Hato nodded slowly. "As long as you and Kiddo are aware and keep your wits about you."

"And make better meal choices," Jingle added. "If your stomach's that upset."

"Oh, of course," Dom agreed. "And soon enough we are going to have a happy little team to watch over us too."

Flip was back in view, yawning and leaving a bowl and a glass by the sink. Kiddo bit a soapy knuckle.

Hato, not noticing Flip had committed such a crime, cleared his throat. "While you're waiting for the team …"

"We should relax?" Dom asked. He examined his wrinkling fingertips.

Hato rubbed his jaw.

"You should do a quiet side job," he said. "And rescue Seethe's therapist."

Making more distressingly wet noises, Dom craned to blink up at Kiddo, surprised. Kiddo was just as speechless.

"Seethe … has a therapist?" Dom asked, somewhat impressed.

"Seethe had a therapist a few years ago," Hato amended. "Now he has a girlfriend."

"Well wowee!" Dom replied. "That sly old dog, I would never have known."

Jingle tossed her hair. "It makes sense. Since when would Seethe leave Hato for an overseas holiday otherwise?" she asked primly, tapping her nails on the dining table. "He was on a romantic getaway."

"Naw, come on, as if you knew, when we didn't," Dom

teased Jingle, who normally surveyed and knew all. Especially after her upgrades to the systems at the base.

"I was the only one who knew," Hato cut off any bickering before it could start.

Jingle crossed her arms, unimpressed.

"Doctor Laine Dean. She was the one who told me Seethe was gone. She's shaken up, but she might have more to tell if she feels safe."

Dom sat up, drawing his dangling leg back into the bath with another plop.

"Ugh," Jingle rolled her eyes.

"Where is Doctor Dean now?" Dom asked. "We'll get her."

"I appreciate it Dominic," Hato said. "You'll have to keep a low profile."

"No, you'll have to utilise the spray function on the smart toilet there first," Jingle suggested. "Or the lady won't be going anywhere with you."

They had barely hung up after Jingle had sent through the address, before Dom's phone was ringing again.

Sparks.

Dom was quick this time, answering her with his camera and a mischievous grin on.

"I *knew* it," Sparks chortled. She was lying on her stomach on her bed, the morning sun from the window behind her making her into a Greek goddess.

And Pash was splayed out beside her in his plush pink dressing gown. His fluffy slippers were kicking about in the air as he took Dom and Kiddo in with delight.

"I knew you had your camera off for a reason," Sparks cackled.

"Is the toilet not a good enough reason?" Dom enquired innocently.

"For most people," Pash remarked. "But you have no shame."

"True," Dom acquiesced.

"What are you two up to?" Kiddo asked, resigned to his lot. He missed his mechanic-ess already. And Pash too.

He had confided in them both over his desire to talk to Dom about going steady. He had agonised over how to do it, whether he would find the words or if he should make some grand gesture, and they had listened and advised.

In the end, Dom had brought it all out of Kiddo in a passionate rush, and it had happened exactly as it should have.

"Sparks is going to help me pack," Pash told him. He pouted and flopped down flat on the bed with a huff.

"He's struggling to narrow things down to the necessities," Sparks explained.

Pash assumed a suffering expression. "Lady Pash has needs."

"Lady Pash and current Pash both have needs," Sparks said. "But at the end of the day you have to be able to navigate underground Tokyo with one manageable bag."

Pash had been saved from the snatcher expo just over a year earlier, owning nothing but the glittering buyer-attracting gown the snatchers had clothed her in. Yet Pash had joined the Raze gang, used Jingle's help to set up a modelling profile, started making a steady income, and had been bringing in mountains of accessories, clothes and cosmetics ever since.

"I'm going to have to wear the heavier things, anyway," Pash remarked. "So that'll save me some bag room."

"Please wear the bulletproof vest Sparks made you," Dom begged. "I've heard all about it."

"Bulletproof *chest*," Sparks corrected happily. She pulled Pash up from her bed, taking the camera and Pash down the hall to Pash's room.

It had been Dom's for a short while, but he was so often away and always strayed into Kiddo's room anyway, so it had made sense to give it to a new recruit.

Now the space was considerably brighter, like the boudoir of a diva queen.

In the corner of the room there stood a seamstress' mannequin, and it wore …

"Aren't they just the loveliest set of coconuts you've ever seen?" Pash gushed.

The bulletproof chest was quite attention grabbing. A pair of pert, very life-like and very naked breasts stood out on the mannequin, in just the right dark, smooth skin tone to suit Pash's.

"It's a faux silicone breastplate, but made with flexible plastic, foam and woven ceramic balls on the inside," Sparks explained proudly. "So lady Pash won't be beeping at the airport in her armour."

"Could confuse the drug scanners though." Pash picked up a big handful of eyeliners and lipsticks, but Sparks shook her head, selecting just two of each.

"Gah!" Pash cried out. "It's my first time travelling overseas of my own free will, and I can't even splash out."

"You think you'll be ready for your flight?" Kiddo asked Pash doubtfully.

So far the bag open on the bed only contained some makeup.

"I'm on it," Sparks affirmed. "Pash is going to be there to represent me too, seeing as I can't come myself." Her face grew solemn, as she thought of Seethe and what the gang might be up against.

"We'll miss you," Dom promised.

"But you and Jingle are kind of the biggest reasons that any of us can be here, or be part of a Raze gang at all," Kiddo reminded her. "There would be none of that, and no saving Seethe, if you two weren't expanding your businesses to support us all."

The Lair club had been enough to provide for Hato's group when they had just been acting as vigilantes in their own area. But once Hato, Dom and Flip had decided to spearhead a real anti-snatcher movement; training and housing recruits, tightening security, planning both local and wider hits on the snatchers, expanding the base with more rooms and a medical wing – the gang had had to work out how to fund that.

Most of the gang members suited and were happy simply as snatcher hunters in the field. And while patrolling had also been a part of Sparks' and Jingle's lives, it was their specific workplace skills that the team had turned to when they had needed to increase their income.

Sparks had taken on apprentices of her own, and was

one of the youngest, yet most sought after car-tists around. She modified, tailor made or restored priceless vehicles like works of art desired by top model buyers and street racers alike. And, perhaps even more successfully, though less well known, she was a custom weapons and defence developer.

This worked well with Jingle's increasingly in demand cyber security business. The sweet lounge singer was now rubbing shoulders with independent business partners, and was securing military and police contracts too.

Interestingly, though almost no surface world elites, government organisations, or even some of street racing gangs, acknowledged Jingle or Sparks' ties to the Raze movement against snatchers … they all seemed keen to prove their support of the right side. Getting into business with Jingle or Sparks, and indirectly supporting Raze, to prove their own lack of connection to anything wrong in the system.

And the jobs had started flowing in.

"Speaking of positives," Pash put supportive hands on Sparks' shoulders. "I think Frazzle is in luuuurve."

"What?" Dom spluttered. "First Seethe has a therapist, *and* a girlfriend. Now our unassuming Frazzle's in love?"

Sparks rolled her eyes. "Pash is trying to predict the future."

"Frazzle employed Doctor Daleeah to work with him," Kiddo explained. "She's the most soft hearted, lady-like bully I've ever met."

She'd personally packed Kiddo's ADHD and epilepsy medication for the airport, with her doctor's note to get him through.

"Two of our guys nabbed *doctors*?" Dom shook his head in admiration. "But the medical wing hasn't been furnished yet. Why has Frazzle employed her?"

"She gave him no choice," Pash sniggered. He picked up a luscious auburn wig, preparing to transform into lady Pash. "She was sick of patching street kids up at the hospital and then sending them off to be at risk again. She heard of a combat medic who had got the right licensing and money to open his doors to those in need. She wanted in on that."

"She's helping him get equipment donated, and to draw up plans for the medical wing's final look as they wrap up construction," Kiddo went on.

"And, Daleeah has a Syrian background. The doc is able to speak to Frazzle in Arabic and help him learn more English," Sparks said.

She had set her phone on the dresser, and was now folding select items of practical clothing to go into Pash's suitcase.

"We already have more young women turning up to the makeshift clinic they've set up, just to chat to a female doctor," Sparks commented with satisfaction. She shook her head once again when Pash held up a very see-through blouse.

"I like her," Pash decided, dumping the blouse. "She wears bright hijabs with floral patterns. And she makes Frazzle smile."

Sparks tutted as Pash threw a loose toothbrush, some underwear and an eyelash curler into the suitcase all in one go.

"I like this Doctor Daleeah too then," Dom agreed. "And am reserving judgment on Seethe's Doctor Dean. Any other big updates I should know? Kiddo always says he has no news."

Kiddo had no defence. He really could never remember any day to day news when asked.

"That's why you should call *me* straight after," Sparks smirked.

"Or meee," Pash added. "Kiddo's such a daydreamy scatter head. And I mean that affectionately."

"Of course," Kiddo accepted that dryly. "Lucky I'm on break now. Exams were not my thing."

His final year had taken every shred of mental capacity and energy to get through. He knew he had brilliance in him, but focusing on a million little boring tasks, and then concentrating on regurgitating the information from the million little boring tasks under pressure had been his fatal academic flaw.

He had made it into culinary school in a round-about way rather than through overall excellence on results day. And the stresses of finding his way, or blindly fighting his way, through the year had consumed most of his mental space.

"Other than all that," Sparks reflected, "your recruits have been missing you here," she told Dom. "Flip is much less patient than you, and Hato is much grumpier. The newbies want you to swap with Flip so he can lead the field teams and you can do the training."

"Hmmmm. What does Flip think?" Dom asked. "It's probably his turn to spread his wings abroad."

"I bet he'd prefer to swap too," Pash smacked freshly glossed, bright pink lips together. "He thinks we're all annoying."

Sparks shook her head adamantly again when Pash questioningly held up some lethal looking stilettos.

"Oh, one more thing!" Pash added, tossing the stilettos back into the cupboard. "I saw some of Start's future plans for development!"

"Hush. It might be a surprise," Sparks warned. She neatly divided the case by placing things more carefully into categories.

"Why, what else are they planning to add to the warehouse?" Dom asked curiously.

Pash clapped in excitement. "Not to the warehouse, but across from it. A restaurant, or diner, or café, or whatever food joint, for Kiddo to run one day!"

Kiddo felt his eyebrows shoot up. "That's a lot of faith that I'll be getting through culinary training. And a business management course too."

"And it's not misplaced faith either," Sparks told him – taking a moment to peer right into the camera. "They see a bright future for you. As do we."

"Now get out of that bath," Pash declared. "You're both wrinkling before my eyes. It's upsetting."

"The water *is* getting cold," Dom admitted. "And I simply must take my boyfriend to bed to consummate."

He smiled evilly as Sparks and Pash both squealed and made to rush to the camera.

He ended the call so that the screen froze for a moment on Pash's hand reaching for Sparks' phone, and Sparks' face over Pash's shoulder.

Dom laughed and peered up at Kiddo.

"Shall we?"

"Our first time as a couple," Kiddo assented.

He reached for a towel.

| 6 |

Six

Kiddo was still adept at surviving on a lack of sleep.

On the other hand, like a viper after not enough zs, Dom just glared dangerously at the bald man they again passed on their way out the next morning.

Kiddo shivered at the mean expression the bald man shot back at Dom, before the man returned to scrubbing the walkway through the emerald tunnel with the crystal blossom trees.

Kiddo remembered that, because of Dom, that man had lost his status, and 'a very important piece' of himself.

Though still bleary eyed, Dom had easily guided them through a maze of tunnels and up a man-hole to surface in a quiet side street. He'd confidently navigated them toward a train station, organising two passes. And Kiddo had watched, fascinated, as the early morning commuters had queued respectfully, waited for disembarking passengers to be off, and then filed into their carriages in an orderly way.

There were no collisions between impatient boarders bowling through those exiting the train, no feet up on seats, no loud phone conversations, and no obnoxiously projected music channels.

Many commuters wore hygienic face masks, and because it was not the right time for Dom to be an easily identifiable target, he was wearing a black face mask himself.

He had donned the fingerless leather gloves that Seethe had once given him to cover the lotus tattoo on his finger, and he had flipped up the collar of his leather jacket to hide any traces of the tattoo edges on his neck.

"Start messaged us this morning," Kiddo told Dom, reaching up to take hold of the roof rail for balance.

"Oh, yeah?" Dom took that as an invitation to lean against Kiddo and shut his eyes.

"He wanted a list of places that we'll be visiting when we put you on exhibition, so that he can work out where our team should be positioned."

"You leave that list of places to me," Dom instructed. "I'll send it through when we're waiting to change over."

It would take two trains and a short walk to find their target. Doctor Laine Dean had, intelligently, not gone back to the hotel she and Seethe had booked.

She had phoned Hato straight away, and was now holed up in a new hotel across town, paid for under a false name through an emergency account that Jingle and Hato had set up for the gang in case of just such an occasion.

Dom perked up a bit when Kiddo bought him a sandwich from a convenience store, and got to work on the list for Start between trains.

Having been banned from seeing the list, Kiddo tilted from foot to foot, taking in everything around them.

The station speakers chimed with a musical sound before each announcement, and most of the station was already quiet and clear of the huge crowds of commuters they'd begun with, who would by now have made it to work or classes. The air was crisp and everything was so clean and ordered. It was lovely.

"You'll never in your life find a better sandwich than a Japanese convenience sandwich," Dom sighed blissfully, pressing send on his list and putting his rubbish in his backpack. "I'm happy now. So, so happy."

"You're a simple creature," Kiddo commended him.

"Simple and satisfied," Dom agreed, putting his mask back on.

"Hato organised for Doctor Dean's bags to be transferred to Blossom at Lotus Bar," Kiddo read out from the group chat. "So we won't be pack mules trying to get her to safety."

"Even better," Dom said. He led the way onto their next train, into a quiet carriage where they could sit down. "But you know what would be the *best*?"

"What would be the best?" Kiddo asked, playing along.

"If we had met up in Tokyo last night on a romantic getaway of our own," Dom sighed dreamily. "To celebrate you getting into your course, and getting through school. Our first trip as a couple."

"Taking happy snaps and hitting the rides at the theme parks?"

"That, and exploring from Tokyo to Kyoto, taking bullet trains for the fun of it, climbing to the top of the shogun palaces. I'd take you to Osaka Castle – my favourite."

Kiddo nodded. "Once we find Seethe, we might have time for those things."

It was nice to think about all of the tough stuff ahead being over.

"Don't you worry," Dom promised. "I've got other plans up my sleeve. We'll be on the job, being noticed. But we'll be having some fun while we're at it."

"No fear," Kiddo answered. "I nearly always have fun when I'm with you, whether we're trying to have fun or not."

"Nearly always?"

Kiddo gave him a dry look. "Being snatched wasn't the best."

He shuddered. The judging, the drugging, the near heart attack, the teeny tiny shorts.

"So true," Dom acquiesced. "But," he waved a pointer finger. "I did give you the best hickey ever bestowed upon any neck while we were down there." He smiled to himself while he reminisced. "I thought that would never go away."

They disembarked when the train had taken them further out from the towering buildings and seemingly never ending views of spires from the cityscape. They weren't quite in suburbia, but the streets were more open and less crowded.

As they left the station, Dom's eyes lit up at the sight of an ice-cream booth.

"We're on the job," Kiddo reminded him with a stern tone. "We're being purposeful and disciplined."

"We're in Japan. We're getting green tea ice-cream," Dom shrugged helplessly. "We have no choice."

Kiddo decided the sugar hit was worth it, and soon they

were strolling down the street with two little cardboard cups of matcha coloured happiness in their hands.

"Wow," Kiddo uttered in delight. "The aftertaste makes you want more."

"Just the right amount of creaminess and just the right kick of sharp tea flavour," Dom answered in contentment, licking the last green remnants from his paddle shaped wooden spoon with relish. "Oh, good! A bin!"

Kiddo realised that the garbage bin beside a street vending machine was one of the first he'd seen in public since arriving. Yet the streets were pristine. None of that urban grit he was used to, where there were bins everywhere and people still couldn't always put the energy into getting to one.

Fascinating.

They found the address of the small apartment building, or ryokan inn, where Doctor Dean was staying, and Dom respectfully made sure all of his ink was still covered before they entered.

"She's ready to go. In the corner over there," Kiddo whispered, gesturing with his chin.

She was waiting for them in the main check-in room, nervously seated by a coffee table with an untouched spread of magazines. She was kneading her palms.

They recognised her by a picture that Jingle had sent – pretty, with a kind face. Small, curvy, and altogether too wholesome looking for the dangerous Seethe.

"I cannot wrap my head around this," Dom whispered back, his lips hidden by his mask.

Doctor Dean's golden blonde curls were tied up into a pretty bun, and her warm red jumper was paired with a pleated grey skirt, patterned tights and lace up, low heels. She even wore small pearl stud earrings.

"How on earth did Seethe nab you?" Dom asked by way of introduction.

She laughed, despite herself, and despite appearing on the brink of tears.

"He said that meeting his family one day would sound a little like that."

Kiddo's gut twisted. Seethe's family.

She held a porcelain hand out, with neat, pink polished fingernails and soft skin. "I'm Laine."

Kiddo took her hand. "I'm Kiddo, and this is …"

"Raze?" she asked very softly, glancing around.

"Where we're going, that's what they call me," Dom agreed. He took her hand too, and pulled her up, into a hug. "You're ok now," he told her. "We're taking you down into a whole new world where nobody can get you."

Laine sobbed a little into Dom's shoulder.

"Thank you," she said in a muffled voice. "But it's not me I'm worried about."

| 7 |

Seven

Laine's face was still splotched with pink patches after crying intermittently throughout the morning. It had been heart wrenching to see her distress.

Kiddo's only solution had been to continuously offer her tissues from a packet that Frazzle's Doctor Daleeah had thankfully tucked into his jumper pocket, in an endearingly motherly way, before he'd left for the airport.

Dom had even decided it was worth stopping at a rescue cat café for lunch, just to make her relax. Laine had managed a smile over the fact that the café's bathrooms had also had a cat or two perched in different places.

Dom had resisted the urge to adopt a cat called Meatball for Miss Lotus, and when they'd left their new feline friends, he'd bought Laine a pearl milk tea to go, and the bubble beads did seem to have cheered her up.

Now Dom led them through some arcade streets, pointing out fun things and being a jolly, though incognito guide.

Kiddo kept reassuringly close to her, feeling somewhat protective of the small, sniffing therapist; stepping tentatively between her two guides as if she expected she was going to be confronted by snatchers again at any moment.

She was a 'civilian'. Not used to the world that Seethe was part of, and was likely in shock.

"Seethe said you were a kid brother to be proud of," Laine told Kiddo thankfully, as she dabbed her eyes with another tissue and sipped at her bubble tea. "He was so upset when you were in danger from the …" she couldn't bring herself to say snatchers.

"By upset, do you mean rip-roaring furious, quietly boiling anger, or downright murderous type of emotion?" Dom joked to lighten her mood.

"Oh no. I've never seen him so flat," Laine shook her head. "Apart from the first time he opened up to me about losing you," she told Dom. "And when you returned he kept your true identity well-guarded from me for a long time to keep you safe."

Dom chuckled. "Lovely Laine, I think you'll find he kept *you* well-guarded from *us* for a long time."

"I'm sure," she laughed shakily. "But I did meet Hato once."

Dom whistled. "Wow, he made you meet the stoic father before the cool siblings. Scary."

Laine stopped him with a gentle hand on his arm. "You know … the night that Seethe did accidentally use your two names in conjunction, so that I guessed you were one and the same, was the night he gave up drinking." Her patchy face was very grave. "He said he could have let such a secret slip to the wrong person, and he could never forgive himself if he did that."

Dom stared.

There were dinging, musical sounds and flashing blue lights from the arcade nearest them, as normal people laughed and played and enjoyed their lives inside.

Dom continued to stare. Kiddo could imagine him gaping behind his mask.

"Seethe *has* been laying off the beers," Kiddo admitted upon reflection. He ran his finger over a large waving cat statue at the shopfront. "The last month or so."

Laine nodded proudly, for a moment even forgetting to eye the streets with anxiety.

It really was a pretty huge step for Seethe, come to think of it. Even if he hadn't announced he was doing it.

"But Seethe is … you know …" Dom winced. "An alcoholic."

"He has been doing wonderfully," Laine assured him.

Kiddo pulled a cringing face over her fluffy curls while her back was turned, and shook his head at Dom. Seethe had been *atrocious* lately. As lethal and bad tempered as ever, and then some.

Dom shook his own head back, in amazement. "You leave base for some international errands, and everything changes. No news indeed," he huffed at Kiddo. "I certainly will be calling Pash and Sparks for the goss in future."

"Change can be such a good thing," Laine told him knowingly. A therapist through and through.

"Well yes," Dom agreed, steering them into a cosy restaurant. The realistic replicas of the food on offer were very appealing in the window. "I mean, just yesterday I made the change to upgrade Kiddo to boyfriend status."

She patted his wrist. "That is lovely!"

The counter inside was round and open in the middle, like in a diner, and a sushi train rotated slowly around it. There were enthusiastic customers perched on every seat, with plates piling up around them as small dishes under plastic covers were scooped off the conveyer belt.

Nobody batted an eye in their direction as Dom casually placed Laine's empty cup on a counter and then brought them to a red door in the corner, marked with an emergency symbol. He opened it, revealing a fire hose wrapped around a red wheel, but then he swung that forward too – the reel making for a kind of handle, and quickly ushered them into the cupboard turned tunnel entry.

Kiddo slid his way down a short ladder, and then turned to help Laine in her nice shoes. Dom closed the cupboard, shutting out the happy chatter, clinks of dishes and aromas of assorted foods. The yellow glow of the restaurant light was replaced with the white glow of Kiddo turning on his phone's torch.

"What if there is a fire in that restaurant?" Laine asked in consternation. "A false wall behind a disconnected hose is quite the worry."

"They also have a legitimate sprinkler system," Dom promised. "The hose is just for show for outsiders. Even the employees would hardly pay it any heed. And any inspectors would know not to."

He started ambling along the tunnel, removing his mask and pocketing it. Laine's little heels tapped along after him.

"So … nobody would be after us or be able to find us down here?" Laine asked uneasily as she kept up. "Would they?"

Dom was moving ahead in search of something. "No, not unless they had a tracker on us!" he answered in a way that was meant to put her mind at ease, but instead made Laine peer about in fear.

"Does anybody have some five yen coins?" Dom questioned, getting out his own torch and peering down side tunnels as they passed them.

"You want all my luck?" Kiddo asked, rifling through his pockets for his loose change.

"Those ones are the lucky ones," Dom acknowledged, and then paused. "Aha!"

He flashed his light so that they could see what he had found. "So lucky, that there are some of these babies available for hire in the buggy bay!"

"Underground golf carts!" Laine stated in surprise. "How clever."

"I chose this route in hopes there might be a few at this end," Dom grinned. "You never know, it's like a trolley bay. If nobody has travelled from the den to this end in a while, there might not always be one parked here."

Kiddo handed over a small handful of coins, and Dom fed them into the side of the front cart.

"In bigger tunnels like this, and on longer routes, they're always a good option," Dom informed them. "And they run on luck. As well as electricity."

He unplugged the hybrid cart from the charging station and the cart purred to life, its headlights flooding the tunnel as the coins chinked into the coin caddy. Dom pulled himself into the driver's seat, and Kiddo helped Laine into the middle before sliding in next to her.

"Miss Lotus thinks of everything," Kiddo commented as they pulled out into the main tunnel again, zipping along on the left-hand side of the path.

"I think this idea was Ryo's, that crafty thing," Dom told him. And Kiddo had to admit, he was grateful not to be traversing the underground for the same distance that two trains had taken them earlier.

Laine shivered beside him as they sped through the tunnel quickly, so Kiddo put a comforting arm around her, and she crinkled her eyes at him with gratitude. He noticed her eyes welling again at the nice gesture, or with worry.

Poor thing.

"Huh," Dom said after a while, and Kiddo noticed that Dom was glancing in the rear view mirror. It was reflecting a strip of light across his eyes.

Kiddo peered over his shoulder in surprise.

Another buggy was coming up fast behind them.

"I didn't get the impression that these were frequently used tunnels," Kiddo commented, suspicion in his tone.

"No. They definitely are not," Dom frowned. Disgruntled.

He shared a glance with Kiddo over Laine's head.

Had they been followed?

Who could have known to be watching Laine's new hotel – which had been so secretly organised?

Why would they have waited to strike?

Dom slowed down and eased off into the next tunnel opening. He brought them to a stop.

"We'll let them go by," he told Laine reassuringly.

Their lights approached, flooding the main tunnel that Dom had just turned off. But the lights did not go past.

The other buggy had stopped.

"Oh no," Laine whispered.

"I'm sure they're not after you," Dom tried to make her feel better. "You've just been in the wrong place at the wrong time twice now."

He and Kiddo stepped out of the buggy, coming together in front of it so that their own headlights were at their backs.

"They could be some of Miss Lotus' people?" Kiddo tried with hope. "Or by chance the tunnels are busy today?"

There was the sound of four sets of feet touching down on the concrete.

There was the distinct flick and click of a blade springing up from its sheath.

The sound of someone else thumping a baseball bat into a palm.

"We'll keep you safe," Dom promised Laine. "And hey," he told Kiddo. "If we survive, we could catch a snatcher for questioning before the team even gets here."

"Grand," Kiddo stated unhappily. "Just grand."

| 8 |

Eight

Laine cried out in fear as the four figures slinked into view.

Three were masked. One, interestingly, had his face confidently on display.

The headlights behind Dom and Kiddo would have been blinding the four wraiths as they approached, but gave Laine a very clear view of the bleeding fang emblems stretching freakishly over the mouths of each of the balaclava covered faces.

"I have not missed that image," Kiddo muttered.

Dom would still be entirely familiar with that garb because of his efforts around the world. But at home, the snatchers had been largely decimated by Hato's Raze gang. They now hunted down only the disorganised snatcher leftovers, and could focus on less local issues.

"Look at the teeth on that one," Kiddo added quietly,

squinting at the one with the threatening smile on show. His canines had been sharpened.

"I'll take the knife, you take the bat," Dom sighed.

The blade in the sharp toothed snatcher's hand appeared more like the kind of small Stanley knife you would use for carving up thick boxes. It was mean, but it would be unlikely to cause fatal damage.

That was odd.

Maybe they were not very experienced ruffians.

Then the four split up to charge at Dom and Kiddo.

Kiddo ducked the baseball bat as it swooshed by over his head. While that snatcher whirled around, Kiddo stayed low and rammed his shoulder into the other weapon-less one, the force throwing that snatcher back against the wall with a crack.

Kiddo grabbed his stunned opponent by the shirt front. He held the giddy snatcher up as a shield in time for the bat wielder to be swinging again. Right into the head of Kiddo's shield.

There was the sound of a baseball bat thudding into a crackling skull. There was a startled curse from the bat wielder. And Kiddo threw his now rag-doll like shield at the baseballer, swiping the bat when the baseballer flinched away from the body of his comrade.

Kiddo was the one to cause the echoing sound of a bat hitting a skull this time. And then he turned to find Dom.

"Oh, thank you for trying to help," Dom was telling Laine. He was helping her to step over the two bodies of his snatchers while she wept. "Please don't do it again though. You seem just as likely to hit me as my attackers here," he jested.

"I'm … sorry," she gasped. "So sorry."

"You didn't mean it," Dom laughed. "It's not like you were trying to kill me. You just jumped on the wrong person's back."

"Oh lordy," Kiddo exhaled in relief and amusement. "Wish I'd seen that."

Dom winced and pressed a hand to his lower back. When he brought it to the light, there was blood on it.

Kiddo hissed and stepped forward, jerking Dom's jacket and t-shirt up to check the damage.

A koi fish above a kidney had been stabbed and de-scaled a little. It was a thumb length gash from the box cutter blade, about two centimetres deep.

"Lucky he didn't get in more swipes," Dom said. "And that he didn't want to carry a more lethal weapon for some reason."

Laine was staring at the sluggishly bleeding cut through her fingers, guilt written across her face. "I'm … so sorry to have caused you harm," she gulped.

"You did not stab me, lovely Laine. It was my decision to turn toward you when you yelled." Dom waved her concern away, pulling his clothes back down. "And I'm more upset that my leather will be damaged. Even if it protected me in the process."

Dom froze then.

He frowned and squinted at the entrance to the main tunnel.

He was gone in a flash, chasing down a new target.

Laine gasped, and Kiddo sprinted after him, in time to

see Dom crash tackling a fifth, also unmasked person to the ground.

Dom slugged the man so hard in the cheek that the man's head was thrown to the side and Kiddo saw him clearly in the headlights.

Kiddo swore.

It was the bald man. Miss Lotus' bitter slave.

Dom raised his fist again.

Punch. "Were you waiting for them to finish us off?" he demanded. Punch. "What are you doing down here?" Punch. "How did you know where we would be?"

"Wait," Kiddo called out over the echoes of Dom's anger. "Give him a chance to talk. He might have information."

"He can't talk, even if he would choose to," Dom spat at the man, whose eyes were now unfixed. "He has no tongue."

"No tongue?" Kiddo was taken aback. "Tongue?"

"Yes, what important piece did you think he was missing?" Dom did pause then.

"Um …"

Dom laughed. "Ohhh. No Miss Lotus only does that to rapists. This guy had been talking to and helping the wrong crowd. Helping sex traffickers but not actually doing the deed himself."

Laine sobbed again, holding herself in revulsion as she stared at the man Dom had caught.

"We might be able to get him to write," Dom shrugged, and climbed off his bald victim's prone body. "But we're leaving him here and getting out of these tunnels, just in case. He won't be up and about for a bit anyway."

Dom took the baseball bat that Kiddo still held loosely in

one hand. Then Dom calmly smashed it into the bald, mute man's legs to make sure.

"Such a shame," Dom shook his head, dropping the bat with a clatter. "This guy is the one Ryo normally calls to clean up messes like this."

Laine was pretty much asphyxiating now, but she followed Dom to some rungs in the tunnel wall that led up to the surface world again.

"You good?" Kiddo asked Dom, noticing that he had slowed right down.

"I'm tired," Dom admitted. "But we'll get a taxi straight to Lotus bar. I'll message Blossom."

Kiddo climbed up the ladder rungs first to move the heavy manhole cover, checking to make sure he wasn't going to surprise anyone and draw attention.

They were in an alley, dusk was setting in, and the streetlights didn't quite reach down their lane, so he reasoned they would be largely unnoticeable in the dim light. He pushed his way out and turned to help Laine up into the street.

He was surprised at how heavily Dom relied on Kiddo to pull himself up out of the hole too.

"I think we're close to the inner city again," Kiddo said, taking the shell shocked Laine by the hand and Dom by the elbow to guide them out of the alley to the street.

They were surrounded by the red, blinking lights of endless tall buildings and towers again. Glittering, bustling city life. Giant screen billboards and brightly lit shopfront windows.

"It won't be a long taxi ride," Dom nodded slowly. "But pricey. You'll need to put it on card."

Kiddo let Dom pause to put his mask back on, and Kiddo moved to the curb to scan the road for a taxi in the traffic.

"Ahh, man," Dom groaned.

Kiddo turned to find Dom now leaning with a hand against the brick wall of the alley.

"You're going to have to text Blossom," he told Kiddo, holding out his phone for Kiddo to take. "I'm going blurry."

"Hail us a cab," Kiddo told Laine, and rushed back to Dom's side.

Kiddo steered Dom to lean back against the wall. He was taking deep breaths, and roughly rubbed at his eyes.

"Do you think …" Kiddo anxiously pulled Dom's jacket around him, adjusting the collar.

"I think I got hit by some kind of snatcher sedative," Dom finished for him. He slurred a little. "I just don't know how. How they knew where she was. To find us."

"It's a slower acting drug," Kiddo glanced back to see that Laine had managed to wave down a taxi. It was pulling up now, its automatic door opening. "I wonder why."

Dom shrugged a shoulder. "Still doing the job. Lucky it wasn't our therapist. Might have been a smaller dose meant for her."

Kiddo sent a speedy text of warning to Blossom and pocketed Dom's phone.

Dom straightened and made to move toward the taxi, but nearly toppled over.

Kiddo caught him and Laine quickly scooted across the back seat to help lever Dom in and onto the middle seat. She was crying once more, eyeing Dom fearfully as the automatic door closed again.

"He'll be ok," Kiddo promised her – hoping he was right. That this was just a typical snatcher sedation scenario. "He's been drugged."

The polite taxi driver nodded when Dom muttered something in Japanese. Street names and directions.

Kiddo bit his lip when Dom gave up then, ripping his mask off and simply laying his head back against the seat, closing his eyes.

"I'm so sorry that this happened," Laine whispered, taking Dom's leather clad hand. She hiccupped. "It's my fault."

"It isn't your fault," Kiddo told her firmly. "We wanted to protect you from something like that happening to you again. We're sorry that it did, despite our efforts."

Laine shook her head, wretched and probably sinking further into her prolonged state of shock.

Incredible mixes of city life and quiet gardens blurred by, and Kiddo pushed back Dom's hair worriedly. Feeling that his brow was cool to touch.

When Miss Lotus' bar came into view, Kiddo was already leaning forward over the front seat to swipe his travel card for payment. The taxi pulled into the curb, its door opening again, and Kiddo levered a frowning, groaning Dom out after himself.

Laine stepped out onto the street on her side of the car, but before Kiddo had finished getting Dom's arm over his shoulder, he heard a squeak of fear from Laine.

"Snatcher," she gasped as a darkly clad figure pressed in at her side.

It was a man in dark clothes, wearing a red hygiene mask

over his mouth, and he simply swept by her to get into the taxi, rather than going in for any kind of attack.

But it was all too much, and the next moment, Laine was crumpled to the road in a faint.

| 9 |

Nine

"You save *her* from getting run over," Blossom's voice announced her arrival. And then she was reaching past Kiddo.

She grabbed for Dom, pulling him toward herself by his belt buckle. She ducked under his arm as if she'd helped a drunken Dom countless times.

Gritting his teeth, Kiddo did as she said and hurried to scoop Laine up from the road.

"Come on," Blossom called over her shoulder, already heading to a side door for the bar.

She pressed her palm to a section on the door, and Kiddo was hardly surprised when it was an invisible panel in the innocent looking wall beside the door that opened instead.

Kiddo had assumed that he was about to be led into Blossom's security domain, but of course it was a blue lit corridor.

He did catch glimpses through thick, glass walled rooms, filled with screens, more flickering blue lights and tech, but Blossom was taking Dom to the end of the corridor, where there was the silver sheen of an elevator. Even as they approached, the elevator opened and brightness poured out around Ryo.

He held the door open for them, taking hold of one of Dominic's arms, and Kiddo grimaced as he angled himself and Laine inside too.

"Should we be taking him down to the den?" Ryo asked Blossom. "It's such a hike."

"I think he's ok to be moved," Blossom answered. "I watched what happened in the tunnels after I got the text. It's not like that time he got back from Moscow."

"And the master will be furious if we don't get him to her," Ryo agreed, adjusting Dom's weight.

The elevator opened, and they were back in the passageway Kid and Dom had accessed from the washing cart door the night before.

"What happened after Moscow?" Kiddo asked, carrying Laine out so the elevator doors shut behind him.

"He took on snatchers who were good with toxins," Ryo answered. "Though fortunately Miss Lotus is even better at antidotes."

"He both won and lost that fight. He made it all the way out of the airport without causing any alarm," Blossom remembered. "And then he'd had enough and we had to do CPR for the whole car ride back here."

"That was the first time in my memory that our mistress chose to come up out of her den to help somebody," Ryo told Kiddo.

They were moving quickly, and were soon back in the wide, white lit tunnels that connected to Miss Lotus' den.

Perhaps they had chosen a quieter entrance, as there were

fewer people around to gawk as they passed, and while they again stepped down a final, emerald green tunnel with crystal blossom trees lining it, they popped out into the garden cavern from a different angle. They were closer to the main house than the tunnel that Kiddo and Dom had used the night before had brought them.

Miss Lotus was seated on the rushes in her main room again, waiting for them with narrowed, unimpressed eyes. Incense smoke curled around her as if her mood had brought a dragon spirit to the room.

Ryo and Blossom lowered Dom to the cushions before her.

Kiddo took the opportunity to set Laine down on a low futon near the entrance, and removed his shoes quickly. Then he crossed to crouch beside Dom.

"Tell me," Miss Lotus ordered Blossom abruptly. Her face was stony.

"He was stabbed in the tunnels by snatchers. They might have been after Raze, or after the lady that Raze and Kiddo were transporting," Blossom reported. "I couldn't get a clear look at the weapon or much else in the tunnels, but on the streets - before they were masked - the attackers looked like they were a European brand of snatcher. Hard to tell what drug is their go-to."

"They used a small Stanley knife," Kiddo supplied.

"Then their choice of a small weapon does suggest they were after short term sedation like usual, rather than maiming and murdering," Ryo surmised with relief.

"They were also joined by a bald man with no tongue," Kiddo added darkly.

Miss Lotus' white eyebrows knitted together. "That *snake*."

"We left him half alive in the tunnels in case you can get anything out of him," Kiddo said.

Ryo straightened. "On it. I'll take care of the clean-up, and then I'll be helping to smuggle your team mates in from the airport," he told Kiddo. "You'll have your network together soon."

Kiddo nodded curtly in thanks.

Ryo bowed to Miss Lotus and left.

"Where did they cut him?" Miss Lotus asked Kiddo with a slightly gentler tone than she'd used for her apprentices.

"Just above the left kidney," he told her. He took a hold of Dom's arm and supported behind Dom's upper back, angling him to sit upward.

Blossom came forward to help draw Dom's jacket off, and then she dragged his t-shirt up and off too. Which might not have been completely necessary, Kiddo thought possessively.

But then Kiddo felt a pang of anguish as Dom's cheek came to rest against Kiddo's shoulder when he was still again.

Goosebumps rose on Dom's skin, and he shivered unconsciously against Kiddo.

"My koi," Miss Lotus lamented. She moved her weight forward, shuffling herself awkwardly to be closer to Dom in the cushions. "He's collected so many more marks on my work."

It seemed that one terrible side effect of the Raze gang weakening the snatcher economy was that they were back to using crude capture methods. The retractable box knife was much less friendly than the autoinjector rings Kiddo's local snatchers had once used.

Miss Lotus examined the rivet that had been made in Dom's skin, which was gaping, but not huge. She checked his eyes and blue tinged fingernails, felt his pale brow and tutted at his slow pulse.

"I've heard of a kind of opioid drug where they purposefully inject the concentrate near a vital organ like the kidneys," Miss Lotus said. "If the organs are slowed right down, so are you. To the point of weakness, lethargy and passing right out for extended times. He would have been incapacitated and unthreatening for quite a while."

Blossom brought forward some clean cloths, a dish of water, a green bottle of what had to be disinfectant, scissors, a needle and thread, a syringe and a vial on a tray.

Miss Lotus selected the syringe and vial, which had a star and an N symbol on it, first. Miss Lotus lined up the vial and syringe, withdrawing the dose, and got rid of any air bubbles. All business, she injected the dose straight into the muscle of Dom's arm.

"Lay him on his side," Miss Lotus told Kiddo. "We'll clean the knife wound while that reverses the opioid effects on his system."

Kiddo levered Dom back downward, and arranged him into a recovery position that would have made Frazzle proud.

"A couple of things are confusing ma'am," Kiddo said, as Miss Lotus wiped at the wound with a wetted cloth, overpowering the smell of incense in the room with antiseptic.

"What is worrying you?" she blotted at fresh darts of blood that rolled over Dom's skin.

Kiddo frowned. "The drug was slow acting. It would have been safer for them to use something that would take him out immediately. And … there should have been no way for them to know where we were in the first place."

Miss Lotus flicked sharp eyes at Blossom, before threading her sterilised needle.

"My team have been checking since I first got the text," Blossom said. "I just got another message to confirm it. Nobody followed Raze and Kiddo from the den this morning. We've scanned the station and train footage and nobody appeared to be following them there either. Even after they reached the hotel, there are also no signs of familiar faces tracking along with them."

"They didn't come from nowhere," Miss Lotus replied, and Kiddo reached to smooth and hold Dom's skin so that she could start her stitches. He appreciated how efficient and neat her suturing was.

"The first that we see them is after you all made a stop at a café," Blossom informed Kiddo. "They just step out of the shadows after apparently surfacing from the actual, official channels under the city."

That meant they had avoided Miss Lotus' passageways as much as possible. Preferring less fun to navigate waterways instead.

Kiddo grimaced in surprise. "I wouldn't have expected snatchers to be hanging around a cat café's pipes by chance."

"A cat café?" Miss Lotus snorted. She tied off her final stitch, snipping the thread free. "Can you recount what happened in there?"

Kiddo watched her dab disinfectant over the now sealed wound again, then use her fan to gently dry it.

"Doctor Dean was quite upset after losing Seethe," Kiddo explained. "Dom and I bought her lunch, she used the bathrooms and Dom grabbed her a drink. Then we headed straight for another food establishment, where we were able to enter the tunnels and hire a buggy. We didn't notice anything wrong until the headlights of another buggy were speeding up behind us."

Blossom moved to hover over the still overcome Laine. She felt for Laine's pockets, and withdrew the therapist's purse. She flicked past a business card pouch, a travel card and a driver's license. Then she checked Laine's phone. "Dead," she mused. "Who knows when it died though."

"We never saw her on it," Kiddo assured Blossom. "She would have spent a fortune calling Hato for help off the street that first night."

Blossom shrugged, still not totally trusting. "Well these snatchers were able to find your location at the cat café quickly, and follow you, unmasked, for about five minutes. They waited a little after you entered the rotation sushi shop. Then I can see them hurrying in. When I swap cameras I can see them dropping down into the tunnel and three of them masking up."

Kiddo remembered the oddly sharp toothed knife wielder.

Miss Lotus pressed an adhesive bandage to Dom's lower back. "I assume they chose their interesting style of opioids," she returned to Kiddo's other point. "Because those drugs won't have damaged our Raze much. It might have been a little slow to have an effect, but it definitely took the fight out of him in the end."

"Even if a bit too late for them to make use of it," Blossom smirked.

Kiddo pressed his lips into a hard line. He undid the studs of Dom's fingerless gloves and pulled them free.

"They likely would have been carrying the same opioid antagonists that I just used, in case they accidentally went too far," Miss Lotus mused. She was feeling Dom's pulse again.

His breathing was like that of one in a normal sleep.

"The dose could have been meant for either Raze or the doctor here though," Blossom frowned. "The way she steps into the frame during the attack – they could have been going after her to finish what they had started with your friend, Seethe. Or they could have somehow known that they had found the real Raze, even despite his precautions today."

"Could the man without a tongue have been directing all of this?" Kiddo asked. "He watched us leave this morning."

"He definitely knew what was going on," Blossom answered thoughtfully.

She was scrolling through surveillance again on her own phone screen now.

"He could have been the one to give word. But I don't know how he pinpointed your location, because he seems to have waited for contact from the snatchers, rather than the other way around. He positioned himself to be cleaning near the main buggy bank, which connects to any of the tunnels you might have come home by, based on the direction you took this morning. But he only high-tailed it into action when he received a call not long after your snatchers showed their faces near the cat café."

"They would have needed his guidance to navigate their way out of our tunnels," Miss Lotus remarked. She was now wiping Dom's brow with a freshly wetted cloth.

Kiddo groaned in frustration. "So we really did miss an opportunity to find out where Seethe is."

"Yet you got the person you went out for, and she's safe," Blossom stated matter-of-factly. "Even if her battery's dead. Now you need to wait for your team so you can do things properly, as planned."

Blossom's eyes lit up then, as her phone pinged. "And this will cheer you up. Ryo has cleaned up down there, and taken care of our snake." She held up her screen so that Kiddo could see a picture. "Does this mean anything to you? It was in his pocket."

It was a business card. Creamy white, but with a bloody fingerprint on it. And while it appeared to have no contact details on it, it did have a shining silver picture of a wolf's head.

"Nope," Kiddo negated. "Not much use without a number or address on it. It's probably more of a call to action or membership card."

Blossom crossed to the wood panel in the wall. The sleek TV eased its way out, and switched on. She was already connecting to a conversation. "We'll ask your friend Jingle to look into it."

"Wait," Kiddo began. "Not while –"

There was a deep horrified gasp from behind Blossom,

and she took a step back from the screen when she saw how intensely close Hato's eye was to the camera.

"What happened?" Hato rumbled.

"He's fine," Kiddo promised. "All patched up. Sleeping it off."

"Tell me," Hato ordered.

Miss Lotus saved the situation. She gave Hato the short, sharp details and he had to respectfully listen.

"Raze and Kiddo brought your Doctor Dean in safely, and my apprentice, Ryo, will soon be co-ordinating one of my teams to pick up yours," she finished. "So all is well."

Flip and Jingle, both in various forms of pyjamas, had pulled Hato back so that all of them were now in the screen.

"I'll look into the calling card," Jingle promised. "And Start is organising some strategies for the team for when Raze is back on his feet and able to be bait safely."

"Which won't be long," Miss Lotus admitted flatly. Still clearly wishing she could hold Dom prisoner with her.

Hato signed off with an unhappy "be careful," to Kiddo.

| 10 |

Ten

Blossom left to fetch Miss Lotus her attendants for the night, and Miss Lotus told Kiddo to wait and to let her helpers transfer Laine and then Dom too.

Instead, she poured Kiddo and herself two small cups of green tea from her tray.

The jade coloured, porcelain teapot had been heating over a candle sized flame, and Kiddo hadn't realised how much he had needed the soothing warmth of that tea.

He sagged a little when he remembered the joyousness of green tea ice-cream with Dom.

"Thank you," Kiddo told Miss Lotus emphatically. "So much – for everything."

He placed his empty cup back on the tray, and took one of Dom's hands, rubbing his thumb along the lotus tattoo on Dom's finger.

"You seem as genuinely attached to him as I am," Miss Lotus remarked with the wisp of a smile.

Kiddo nodded. "He is one of the only people who gives me everything I need."

"Ah yes. He is addictive," Miss Lotus remarked.

"He is like a shot of light," Kiddo replied. Then felt his cheeks flush.

Miss Lotus nodded slowly. "He has brought me much light in the darkness too."

Kiddo noticed that the warm, golden lamps in her main room were becoming especially ambient. The bright garden spotlights were likely being wound down and the lanterns and fires lit around the outside again.

"Can I ask," Kiddo paused, hesitating. "What was it that he did to capture the heart of one who is so powerful?"

Miss Lotus smiled a slow smile. "One who is so untouchable and formidable, you mean."

Kiddo winced. "You do good things. But you *are* frightening. And while many pay respects to and follow you … I didn't get the impression that you had many you felt 'genuine attachment' for."

She didn't seem particularly insulted by his honesty.

"I feel affection for my apprentices, though I am tough on them," Miss Lotus answered thoughtfully, as if she hadn't really considered it before. "I am pleased by my consorts. And I am largely unbothered by my followers if they are living by the right code."

"But Raze is different?"

She pursed her lips. "He made me love him despite myself. His cavalier attitude, and his willingness to do anything for a friend. He decided *I* was a friend worth having." She reached forward with an awkward effort on her folded legs, raking the loose flicks of Dom's hair back from his face. "And I hadn't known I'd needed one."

"When he finds his kind of people," Kiddo agreed. "He does whatever he can for them."

"And for once, someone was weaselling their way in here without any desire for personal favour, power, training or advantage. I didn't do anything for him, he simply kept sneaking in here to keep me company. Out of curiosity, and then care." Her voice was withering but her eye-lined eyes were kind.

"It's a wonder Blossom and Ryo weren't horrified at the breach of security," Kiddo commented.

"Oh, they were stupefied. I berated them, but I didn't order them to try to stop him," Miss Lotus answered. "For a brief time they were even jealous of him – stealing my time and me letting him. But then they came to know him. They followed him when he wasn't in here with me. And they saw what kinds of things he was getting up to."

"He let them follow," Kiddo asserted.

"Probably right," Miss Lotus accepted that. "Because it got him what he wanted. They became his little helpers on different occasions."

Miss Lotus nodded at Laine as two guards in red uniforms came to bow in the doorway.

"Her first. One of the tents is for her," Miss Lotus instructed.

Kiddo hadn't even noticed any tents when they'd hurried back into the vast den. But Miss Lotus had said Dom's friends could stay, and she must have made room for them.

She rubbed at her kimono, as if her curled up legs were sore, as she spoke to Kiddo again.

"Yet, Raze is also special because, in the short time he was here, he helped me to achieve closure over two very important things in my life."

Her dark eyes glittered on Kiddo, and he was mindful that he was somehow being deemed worthy of this woman's time too. He was aware that he was incredibly fortunate.

"The first thing, was my legs," Miss Lotus explained, and Kiddo frowned, confused.

With a sinking feeling, he realised what her rounded shape, her discomfort and her tucked kimono might mean. That her legs were not simply folded beneath her.

"Were you snatched?" Kiddo asked sickly. "They did something to you?"

She shook her head. "No child. Terrible people can exist in the world without being part of the snatcher organisation. A few drunkards, barely older than I was, accosted me when I was a teen. I was half alive when they were done, and threw me on the train tracks. But not far enough onto the tracks."

Kiddo realised that he was kneading Dom's hand between his now, and he made an effort to stop. Swallowing.

"I lost my legs instantly, but they were cauterised instantly too," she stated matter-of-factly, before she left that topic. "I had been training as a geisha, you know. I was young and promising. And I didn't give it all up, but I did decide to leave that whole world. I built my own down here, and became more of a fascination – a sought after, hidden rarity. Those in the know splashed money to be allowed to meet with me, and I used that money to grow my own investments and spread my tentacles. All while I made my den into everything I loved most."

She shrugged a strong shoulder then.

"But Raze knew I needed more for closure than power and admiration," she said seriously. "When I told him my story, he didn't come back for nights," she explained. "And when he did … he brought me the heads of my attackers."

Kiddo gaped.

"Oh I know, it's archaic and messy," Miss Lotus' lip sneered with evil pleasure at the memory. "But it was exactly what I needed."

"… How …?"

"He got Blossom to go through old police records, and Ryo translated it all for him," Miss Lotus answered. "He went door knocking on every witness' house. Used some neck trick or other to scare them. And all he had to do was find *one*. One now enfeebled person who knew more than they'd said in the past – or who had *one* more than they'd said. Then that witness became Raze's suspect, and led a trail to the others."

She tilted her head, her eyes remembering.

"Their faces were so much older. So, so much older. But I could see my attackers in them."

"And the second thing?" Kiddo half whispered. "The second thing you needed closure for?"

Her face became like stone. "My daughter."

The guards were back, but were waiting respectfully outside for Miss Lotus to be ready.

"I was a wealthy curiosity of the underworld. She was a prize. I let her live in both worlds, to her ruin." Miss Lotus straightened. "That one was snatchers. And she was already long dead before Raze, or even Blossom and Ryo had come along. My new children. But Raze saw to it that I added over ten more heads to my collection, from those who had been most closely involved in her disappearance."

Kiddo just shook his head – gutted for this empress beneath the world.

"I am sorry." He managed quietly at last. "Thank you for telling me."

"Yes, well, if he has to live up there in that world," Miss Lotus answered. "I am comforted to know that you exist up there too." She gestured for her helpers to approach.

Kiddo let out a pent up breath, eyes down. "I think I'm in love with him."

"Oh yes," she answered. "Most people who aren't afraid of him are. And sometimes even then."

Kiddo winced, nodding.

He'd known as much.

Her guards knelt down beside her. Waiting to lift her up.

"But the difference is, that I think he is in love with *you* too."

| 11 |

Eleven

Kid started awake.

It was still artificial darkness outside, and he had long ago heard their team arrive and quietly sink into their rows of tents in the field beside the lagoon.

Kiddo hadn't moved to greet them, because he'd been sitting on the cottage's low couch, with Dom's head cradled on his legs.

Kiddo had kept Dom laid out across the couch on his side, and he had been mindlessly tracing Dom's bare arms and shoulders – probably to soothe himself more than the sleeping Dom.

At some point, Kiddo must have nodded off, his head tilting back against the thin cottage wall.

But ... now Dom was laying on his back. He had reached one arm up to wrap a hand around Kiddo's bicep.

His blue eyes were clear and bright even in the dim light.

"Hey," Dom smiled slightly. "You ok?"

"I'm fine now," Kiddo whispered back. "Completely good."

"Thank my lucky stars," Dom smiled a little wider, stealing

one of Sparks' sayings. "That neither of us got our throats slit before we got to live the list I sent to Start."

"Thank my lucky stars they just wanted to jab you with a drug," Kiddo added seriously. "Be careful of your back."

"Mmmm," Dom nodded. "Also lucky that Miss Lotus is good with all kinds of needling."

Kiddo interlaced his fingers with Dom's.

"Miss Lotus told me what you did for her."

"She did huh." Dom tilted his head dreamily. "I want to do the same for Seethe and Hato. I think their past owners were too rough and lowly to have been at our first snatcher expo. That event wasn't really for the scum who take power from the fringes. And now that Jingle has some police and military friends, she could check it out again for me."

"Take it easy," Kiddo suggested. "How 'bout we get through what's left of tonight first?"

"Great idea," Dom agreed.

He sat up, swivelling quickly and straddling Kiddo.

"Woah," Kiddo managed.

"I'm a smooth crusader after a good sleep," Dom simmered. He kissed Kiddo's neck and behind his ear. Along his jaw. One hand still interlocked with Kiddo's, and the other grasped Kiddo's jeans button.

It was with Herculean effort that Kiddo pressed Dom back, with Dom only breaking from his kisses at the growing pressure on his sternum.

"What you need is more sleep," Kiddo told him. "You have a big day ahead tomorrow."

Dom gripped Kiddo's hair, turning Kid's head to expose his neck again. Going back in for the kill.

His kisses eventually dragged raggedly and then languidly at Kiddo's lips too.

Kiddo took hold of the backs of both of Dom's legs, which were hemming him in against the couch.

Gripping Dom's legs, Kiddo stood.

"Kinky," Dom chuckled. "Throw me against a wall. But a wooden one, not a screen one."

Instead, Kiddo slowly released Dom to set his feet on the floor. He looped his hands around Dom's waist, and pulled him close.

"Alright, just as good," Dom nodded. "We can work with this. Say something sexy."

Kiddo quirked an eyebrow. "Water."

That pulled Dom up short.

"Water? Interesting choice."

"What do you think of when I say water?" Kiddo inquired knowingly.

Dom sighed, and sagged a little against Kiddo.

"Thirst. Terrible, terrible thirst."

Kiddo nuzzled Dom's shoulder. "And what would you say if I asked you to describe your head?"

Dom put his hands on Kiddo's torso, gripping the material of Kid's tee.

"I would say … just a teensy bit dizzy."

"Ahuh," Kiddo encouraged.

"And maybe still tired." There was resignation in his voice.

Kiddo gently guided Dom around the screen that offered privacy for the bed.

"I would applaud your honesty," Kiddo told him. "And I would tuck you in and get you some water."

Dom begrudgingly, and now slightly gingerly, slid under the covers; carefully settling onto his back.

Kiddo poured him some water.

"So sensible," Dom grumbled crossly. Before downing half a glass, and giving Kiddo the other half. "So unlike me."

"Perhaps it was all a dream," Kiddo shushed him, sliding in and tucking his arm under Dom's neck on the pillow.

"I'm going to finish it differently in my head now," Dom told him. "It'll be better."

"Good idea," Kiddo answered. "I'll do the same."

"I won't be held accountable for any odd noises or movements."

Kiddo kissed Dom's temple.

"Of course not. You can't be blamed."

| 12 |

Twelve

Kiddo stumbled to the door when there was a knock the next morning.

"Oh good, you're already up and dressed," Quicklips beamed, slapping Kiddo on the back in greeting. "How's our resident Raze after last night?"

Kiddo yawned, peering down at his slept in jeans and rumpled t-shirt.

"He needs to pee," Dom moaned back. "And he feels hungover. Go away."

"You've got five minutes," Trix called from her tent. She was setting up a laptop screen to connect with Start and the others. "Then we're planning your day with or without you."

Kiddo could see that Miss Lotus was an extremely generous host to those she let into the fold. Each of the tents were circular and spacious, like glamourous tee-pees. There were trays of food and tea inside each, as well as a wash basin, privacy screen and low bed for each person.

Pash was laying on Trix's bed, despite having a perfectly good tent of his own.

Kiddo could see Tiny in his tent, shaving in a mirror.

Velvet's door was still firmly tied shut.

And Laine, small and blonde and in a holiday maker's carefree pink dress, was sitting with a million cares on her low shoulders. She was out on the lush grass between Dom's cottage and the tents, where there was a clear little glade for them to all sit in together. But rather than looking like she was hopeful and relieved at the gathering to save Seethe, she appeared nervous of the tough, assorted people around her. She was hugging herself.

Dom blinked up as Kiddo came back in; one eye and a wisp of black hair visible from his blanket cocoon.

"I'll meet you out there, ok?" Kiddo grinned.

He washed up and pulled on some fresh clothes before pouring a new glass of water for his medication. Then he set the half full glass beside the bed. "Hydrate."

Kiddo, minty fresh and glad to see his gang, sat beside Laine on the grass to try to reassure her too.

"Is … Raze alright this morning?" Laine asked Kiddo with a shaky smile. "I wasn't too helpful last night." She smoothed her pink dress and pulled her creamy cardigan about herself.

Kiddo patted her on the shoulder. "He'll be out, bright eyed and bushy tailed any minute. And I think you needed the time to recover from all of your shocks and misadventures yourself."

Quicklips sauntered over to join them on the grass. He offered Laine a radiant beam, but she flinched a little at his size.

"Hato said to ask," Quicklips continued to beam brilliantly, "if you are taking your meds."

Kiddo rolled his eyes, but he wasn't insulted. He'd been getting better and better since leaving the cloud of befuddlement he'd been living under for exams, yet Hato would always be the concerned father.

"Ahuh," Kid answered. "Washing behind my ears and eating my vegetables too. He could have asked me himself over our calls."

Velvet pushed through her tent door then, and stalked across to Quicklips' other side.

And if Quicklips' size had seemed intimidating, Laine huddled closer to Kiddo in ruffled uncertainty when she was touched by the rippling waves of frost that always radiated from Velvet.

Velvet didn't even sound a greeting. Just a curt nod at Kiddo. Her dark eyes sharp and her posture as closed as ever. It was a wonder the grass she sat on didn't recoil in fear.

They heard Tiny swearing like a sailor then, before he came stomping out with some squares of tissue pressed to the bleeding spots on his face. Aftershave wafted from him like an invisible weapon.

"Mornin," Tiny muttered, and then flounced down with a scowl.

"Our team dynamic must be an absolute dream to analyse, ey doc?" Quicklips joked, elbowing Laine good naturedly.

She was practically pressed to Kiddo's side now.

"Yes, fascinating," she managed.

So she had analysed everything right.

It was so hard to imagine such a soft lady not fainting on the spot instead of *ating* Seethe. But maybe her timid nature was what was good for him.

"Get out here," Trix called toward Dom's door. "We're ready."

She brought the laptop over to the raggedy semi-circle and perched it on a log stump to get a good view of everybody on the camera.

This time the screen was divided into separate windows, because Jingle had probably tired of squeezing next to Hato.

Start was in the library on the upper level – the light kept changing on his face as he surfed through different tabs.

Jingle was in her office, sipping a night time tea and scrolling through her socials.

Hato was at the kitchen table, experimenting with moving the laptop closer and then further away from himself so that he didn't fill the whole picture with just his head. When Hato pushed it too far away, Kiddo caught a glimpse of Duncan Jr. still alive and well, so Frazzle or Doctor Daleeah must have been feeding the fish as promised.

And even better, Flip was on the ground level, moving around to pack up the training area, and Kiddo kept catching glances of Sparks in her adjoining workshop.

He blew Sparks a mental kiss.

"You're wearing my lipstick," Velvet finally spoke to accuse Pash in a waspish voice.

"Sure am, doll," Pash replied as she approached with a catwalk strut. "If it looks that good on your skin tone, it was bound to suit mine."

Pash was right. The red was striking against Velvet and Pash's midnight colour. But while Pash's lips created a voluptuous, saucy, upward turning pout, Velvet's mouth made a fierce red slash shape right now.

Aside from the vibrant makeup, Pash had gone for a more toned down lady Pash today. With military style cargo pants and lace-up combat boots, and shaven head left bare, but with her rather eye catching protective figure enhancer out on show – loud and proud.

"Morning, sweets," Pash kissed Kiddo on the cheek and took the free spot on Kiddo's other side. "That's from Sparks."

He smiled. She'd sent a kiss right back.

"Is Dominic alright?" Hato's voice projected much too loudly from the laptop, crackling with the volume.

Flip nearly dropped his phone and an armful of marker cones. "Woah. No need to yell, big man," he winced. "They can hear you."

"You'll burst my speaker," Start grimaced, well and truly startled into focusing on only their chat window now.

"Dominic is just dandy, thank you."

Dom had finally wandered out in still just his worn jeans from the night before. He didn't mind that Kiddo had people on both sides. He simply flopped down to lounge with his bare top half across Kiddo's lap and his legs across Pash.

Pash pulled Dom's feet up into her lap so they were cushioned.

"Can you look more alive?" Hato restrained his voice a little, so that it didn't echo around the whole cave now.

"This is the best I got," Dom humphed. But he did tilt onto his side so that he could look directly at the screen and their present gang members – making an effort at the sound of the strain and concern in Hato's voice.

"That poor koi fish," Pash tutted as she saw Dom's back.

"Get us started Jingle," Trix said, affirming that they were all listening and ready now. "What did you learn about the calling card left on the attacker last night?"

There was a clank as Jingle set her mug down. She clicked on something and a photo of the creamy card with the silver sheened wolf's head, taken from the tongueless bald man, opened on the screen. It reduced Hato, Start, Flip and Jingle's images down to a corner.

Laine had covered her mouth as she gazed at that card with its bloody fingerprint.

She was so gentle and disturbed by blood. *So* opposite to Seethe.

"The wolf's head is printed on with a pattern," Jingle said. "It's not just a logo, but like a barcode you can scan with your phone. And then it gives your location to the code's creator, without leaving a trace of the phone contact having happened."

"Clever," Flip's voice puffed as he dragged equipment to a cupboard. "Whoever it is never has to give their own address."

"Yes," Jingle affirmed. "The card means instead they'll find *you*. Which suits the name I have found for them."

"Snatchers are snatchers," Tiny grumbled. "Why do these ones need a fancy name and card?"

Jingle had a slightly concerned expression. "I couldn't find much out. Just rumours. So I don't fully understand it myself," she admitted. "But they are a very new group called The Hunt. And I have a bad feeling that it's our fault they suddenly exist."

"What were the rumours you heard?" Hato asked stiffly.

Jingle closed the image of the wolf so that all of the speaker tiles enlarged again.

"I heard that The Hunt is made up of elite snatchers, coming from the best that each surviving snatcher city can offer," Jingle answered.

"Before last year there were one hundred and ninety four snatcher bases around the world. Now there are one hundred and eighty eight. With more Razes in training for a long future of battling human trafficking," Velvet simmered. "So we forced them to unite out of fear."

"They want to hunt us down," Quicklips guessed. "Not great for us. But it does make sense."

Start was tapping his chin. "Their major problem right now is buyers. We wiped out and exposed so many of their most esteemed buyers, that they'll be searching for a way to reassure new or surviving clients that we won't be a threat. Regular snatching business can be re-established while The Hunt deals with us."

"What better way to deal with us and make buyers happy," Trix mused, "than to take down the Raze founding forefather. The one Raze who apparently frequents Japan."

"Poor Seethe," Laine sniffed. "They got the wrong Raze."

Kiddo noticed that Dom's hand was stopping his own hand from unhappily pulling out clumps of grass.

Miss Lotus wouldn't like that.

"Being Raze got him in trouble. But now it is also the very thing keeping Seethe alive," Start told Laine. "I'm sure they would not have kept his death quiet if they had killed him. They think they can get some other use from him, if he's not the original Raze to kill to send a message."

"Doctor Dean, would you mind recounting the night that Seethe was snatched again?" Hato asked in his most kindly voice. "If we go over the facts we might pick up on something."

Laine drew in a deep breath.

"Of course."

She stared at her hands as she spoke. Her sweet coral pink nails.

"We had spent our first whole day at the happiest place on Earth," Laine said brokenly. "I was wearing a headband with the ears. He was carrying our keepsake popcorn containers. We were tired, but deliriously happy, walking back through the streets without a care. The streets here feel so peaceful and safe."

"They usually are," Dom agreed in a flat tone.

Again, it was just so hard to reconcile a description of 'deliriously happy' with Seethe. It was heartbreaking that she was in her holiday dress and he was on his first romantic joy trip, only for it to have gone like this.

"I of course never picked up on it when the tone changed," she admitted sadly. "But I remember he glanced over his shoulder a few times, and became a bit quiet. Then he was pulling me down noisier streets and I thought he just wanted to check out the bustling stalls that were open so late."

Kiddo started tracing one of Dom's dragons dejectedly. Seethe had *not* been drawn to the late night shopping.

"Suddenly he was knocking the ears off my head and he'd found a beanie from somewhere," she said.

The gang shared looks. 'Found' was a very generous word choice.

"He was pulling my pink cardigan off and zipping me into a new jacket even as we walked. I was so confused. And then he let go of my hand and pushed me down a side street." She shook her head, her curls wisping about. "I was stunned, but he cast an eye back over his shoulder and then sprinted … and a group of thugs I hadn't even seen on the other side of the road sprinted after him. I stumbled out in time to see them all round a corner away from me, and a black, unmarked van was cruising along after them."

"He was taken in the main streets," Quicklips shook his head and slapped an incredulous hand on his knee. "So brazen."

"The popcorn containers were the only thing left, spilled out across the pavement, when I reached the street he'd sprinted down," Laine said in a thick voice. "And then I remembered that Seethe had given me Hato's number for if there was ever an emergency. So that's when I called."

"You called immediately?" Tiny rubbed his jaw, then remembered his stinging spots.

She kept her eyes down. They were red rimmed.

"I … I maybe fled in a panic at first. And wandered around lost and in shock for a bit," she admitted. "I didn't know whether to search the number of the Tokyo police, or if that would make things worse. I couldn't tell which street they'd headed down or what direction. Nobody around me seemed to have noticed. I didn't know whether I should even go back to our hotel."

"I'm glad you called me," Hato told her. "*We* have to deal with this. And we have to deal with this now. Seethe's been with them for three nights."

"I'm messaging each team member as we speak," Start jumped in then. "Each team member has the complete itinerary, down to the minute, for today, as well as instructions for exactly where they should walk between locations or stand when on location in order to be close-by and out of view. You can't interact with each other or be too visible at any point."

"Which means you will need to specifically know where the others are being positioned too, so that you *can* keep eyes on each other," Hato asserted.

Flip was leaning against a car beside Sparks now so that she could listen in. "They'll be able to message over the chat, though, won't they?" he asked.

Jingle nodded. "Our chat is firmly encrypted. You can use it for emergencies, to touch base, or to signal for help subtly."

"My message hasn't arrived yet," Tiny grumbled, as everyone else pinged around him. "The group chat isn't working."

"You're still with that cheap provider," Jingle accused. "I told you to switch out from them. They're literally called Cheapies."

"I'm with them too," Laine admitted, seeming downcast that even her phone connection was feeling fragile. "My phone worked on the surface and in the other tunnels, but not in here."

"See?" Tiny said. "I'm not the only Cheapie."

"Ugh," Jingle rolled her eyes. "You're so cheap you can't get reception beyond a level down. So primitive."

"Are you going to be up for the day ahead Dom?" Sparks cut in then.

She was peering at how thoroughly flopped and immovable looking he was.

"I'll be fine to head out after a quick wardrobe change," Dom promised her winsomely. "My friend Ryo messaged me on my highly receptive phone. He said he left me some hangover curing electrolyte drink in the bar fridge up top."

Dom made the effort to sit himself up and be less flopped and immovable.

"You'll be safe down here," Kiddo promised Laine. "And we won't be coming back until we've found a snatcher who can tell us what we need to know."

Laine squeezed Kiddo's hand in thanks.

"Alright then," Trix announced. "Let's go over the itinerary and get to know our stations while pretty boy puts himself together."

"Naw," Dom stood stiffly. "You think I'm pretty."

"Of course," she snorted. As if it were obvious to everyone in the world. "Tiny, you'll have to read on with someone else until your message comes through when we're higher."

Pash and Kiddo rose too, while the others headed to pack any final necessities or began reading through Start's plans.

Pash gave Dom a kiss on the cheek, as she had for Kiddo earlier. "From Sparks," she said graciously.

"Exactly what I needed," Dom sighed. Then he poked Pash in the sternum; beyond impressed. "You wore your bullet proof chest. It's tremendous."

"Let's get you ready," Pash grinned, linking arms with Dom and Kiddo. "And then electrolyte you up."

| 13 |

Thirteen

Is there anything that Dom doesn't make look good? Pash's text vibrated in Kiddo's hand.

Dom had been still for approximately three minutes before they'd left, leaning against the Lotus Bar and swigging nasty hydration concoctions. Simply because Dom hadn't swatted her away, Pash had smudged a line of smoky liner under Dom's eyes 'for his big day'.

"War paint," Pash had announced.

And Dom honestly had looked like a rock star.

Now the team were pretty much invisible as Kiddo walked the streets, hand in hand with that rock star.

Trix: this chat group is for emergencies.

Tiny: I'm receiving great coverage up here. Getting all messages. Nothing Cheapie about it.

Velvet: I can't believe you used my lipstick. It better be back in my case Pash.

Pash: ...

"I knew your eyes would light up if I showed you a whole roof of Duncan Juniors," Dom grinned at Kiddo.

They were at the foot of an outdoor walkway, and the entire walkway was under hundreds of strings of silken fish kites, blowing about as if they were swimming.

"Did … you make this whole day into one big fun date?" Kiddo asked.

Tiny: ₊i₊ Dom make this whole ₊ay into one big ₊umb ₊ate? We're working here.

Pash: aw, they look like Duncan Jr.

"You and I are going to enjoy ourselves as a couple," Dom said. "But our enjoyment spots are also very intentionally, publicly geared toward our team goal."

They followed the walkway up to a shopping centre complex, which was busy with mid-morning shoppers.

Quicklips: Got₊am. Who puts an amusement park in the mi₊₊le of a shopping strip?

Pash: a genius.

Trix: stea₊y. Hol₊ the lines.

A rollercoaster filled with delightedly squealing people, despite it being mid-week and early morning, raced around the outside of the complex, and also sped through various holes built into the buildings.

A merry-go-round sang its upbeat tune and rotated on the ground level, lit with golden lights. And kids bounced up and down a lane of water, laughing and splashing, encapsulated in giant plastic balls of air.

"I hope you don't mind, but that one is our speed for today," Dom told Kiddo, nodding toward a slow moving Ferris wheel that towered over everything. "That's where I can start spreading the word."

Kiddo shook his head in admiration. "You are so good at this dating thing. Even in the middle of a crisis."

"Unfortunately we seem to have chosen a crisis prone life," Dom answered, leading him up an escalator to join the queue for the wheel. "So I'll always make an effort as your partner, whether we're in a crisis or not."

Dom cheekily grabbed Kiddo's face and drew him into a dip and kiss when the ride photographer took their touristy snap.

Tiny: why'd I have to get the vantage point overlooking the ride lines? So mushy.

Velvet: I'm stationed beside the toilets. Shut up you idiot.

Pash: they kissed for the ride photo, didn't they?

Pash: I bet they did.

Pash: I'm near the store at the exit. I'll buy the keepsake kiss pic.

When they neared the front of the line, Dom appeared to spot someone he was after. He stopped and pretended to need a moment, ushering other passengers ahead in the queue.

"Blabs?" Dom called out in overdone shock. "Blabs, is that you?"

A young man in a bright blue polo top, working the lines, turned at once.

He seemed ready to die of embarrassment.

He politely bowed and greeted Dom in a way that suggested he was going for a 'nice to see you, sir," kind of tone. His eyes darted to the sides at his blue shirted co-workers.

Dom tsked. "No need to be so formal, my friend!" He reached over the barrier to shake 'Blab's' hand, but seized it and pulled the young man closer. "Though there *is* a need for English. This is my boyfriend, Kiddo."

Blabs' face reddened, and he eyed Kiddo uncomfortably too, as if the pair of them had come to his Ferris wheel to jump him.

Dom's friendly hold shifted to Blabs' shoulder, near his neck. And Blabs changed from red in the face, to green. So maybe his fears were right.

"It has been so long," Blabs commented weakly, but respectfully. "Raze."

"Darn right it has!" Dom crowed, messing Blabs' hair. He was drawing attention from all over. "You should meet us for a drink tonight, at our favourite alley in our favourite bar."

"I'm not so good as you," Blabs straightened his hair with a strained smile that kept wobbling. "It's so hard to get in for someone like me. But I'll keep in mind that you'll be there."

"Didn't I always get you in? But yes, keep in mind that I'll be there," Dom agreed good naturedly, releasing his hold and stepping back toward a slowly arriving Ferris wheel capsule. "You do owe me a drink at the very least!"

Blabs blanched. The capsule doors sealed, and Kiddo and Dom were ensconced in peaceful music as they were lifted away from the fearful youth.

"I'm guessing that was not as friendly as it sounded?" Kiddo enquired.

Quicklips: wow, that young dude has just high tailed it right outta there.

Pash: nearly hit me on my way to pay for the photo. Which is super cute btw.

Trix: focus.

Dom settled back and put his arm around Kiddo's shoulders. The view of the shopping centre broadened beneath them, and the city skyline opened ahead.

"Good old Blabbermouth," Dom sighed. "He used to drink with Ryo and I quite frequently in one particularly intimate bar. He would name drop all sorts of dastardly people he rubbed shoulders with through his father's connections. All people we would promptly check out. Until Blabs' father realised exactly who we were, what we might be up to by drinking with his son, and how much we might be worth. Nearly got Ryo killed."

Kiddo raised his eyebrows. "What were a bunch of underagers doing hanging out at a pub all the time?"

Dom kissed Kiddo's knuckles.

"Oh, Ryo and I were there especially because it was the kind of place that gives you up close and personal contact with interesting people. When they didn't know us we learned a lot, even without Blabs' help. But it will be very handy to go there now with them knowing exactly who I am. Telling Blabbermouth should mean his father finds out I'll be there, and he should have some real contacts. As well as a healthy desire to punish me."

Kiddo leaned into Dom's hold, relaxed and enjoying the view. "What exactly did you do to Blabs to make him so hesitant to join you for another drink?"

Dom shrugged. "I was pretty good about it. I gave him a temporary neck adjustment. Scared him back into line – or out of alignment – for just a few minutes. If Ryo had bled out that night, it would have been a much less temporary adjustment."

"You're such a fiend."

Dom smiled, kissing Kiddo's cheek this time. "I know. It's my line of work."

Pash: omg guys. Go for a second ride. I can't get enough of these manga girls. I could eat them up. It's like they've walked out of a cartoon.

Trix: everyone confirm, they're all clear to exit and move to the next location.

Velvet: clear.

Quicklips: a-ffirm.

Tiny: good to go.

Pash: srsly. Guys. They have bows and petticoats.

Trix: ...

Pash: all good.

Next Dom relocated them to the busiest intersection in the world. He put his jacket around Kiddo's shoulders and rolled up his t-shirt sleeves. A nineteen-fifties biker heart-throb.

They joined the chaos of a large crowd waiting at a diagonal crossing, and Kiddo noticed that some people went to the effort to jostle Dom slightly less, as if touching the skin of his arms was a bad idea.

An elderly woman shook her head at his clearly Japanese ink. Others openly stared at it, admiring it. A few youths took sneaky pictures. And many people went out of their way to studiously ignore it.

Kiddo thought he saw perhaps one or two people become warily, but keenly, interested. They possibly knew enough about the underground world, and recognised what that specific ink could mean.

"Here we go," Dom told Kiddo, tightening his hold on Kiddo's hand.

Then the lights changed and pedestrians flooded across the diagonal crossing as if the whistle for a race had just been blown.

The sweeping movement of the crowd felt non-stop, as if the number of people who needed to cross the road was endless. Until suddenly their time was up and they had to be confined neatly, and tightly, to the pavement once more.

Kiddo enjoyed every minute as they leap frogged from crossing to crossing, laughing at the stop-start waves of action and inaction.

It was the perfect way to be exposed to countless people.

Pash: Was that fun? I'm a bit jelly.

Quicklips: Forget jelly. Look what they're eating now.

Pash: Omg, is that nice? It's green.

Dom had found them an ice-cream stand while they waited for word to hopefully spread.

"Tell her it's sooo nice," Dom smiled evilly. Licking up an icy green tea drip.

Pash: wahhhh.

Trix: Tiny and I are going to investigate some observers you've collected. Stand-by.

Kiddo tried not to crane his head to search for them.

Tiny: false alarm – just a perve. So hard to tell when not in masks.

Velvet: were we meant to be reporting false alarms? I think I just beat up a jerk on the corner. Not a trafficker. Regular jerk.

Trix: ...

Velvet: two snatchers on the way to the crossing too. But ordinary snatchers. They knew nothing about wolves and hunts.

Trix: ...

Velvet: I did ask them. Multiple times.

Trix: right.

"I can feel her annoyance rolling out of your phone," Dom sniggered, reading over Kiddo's shoulder.

Trix: anyway. Same scenario here. No luck. They're too low to know what's what. Please report next time.

Dom wiped at Kiddo's bottom lip and then licked his thumb.

"I sure am loving dating you."

Trix: alright. Everyone confirm they're clear to move on.

Velvet: clear.

Quicklips: a-ffirm again.

Tiny: we're good.

Pash: yup. Hey, I think I want to buy a petticoat. Thoughts?

Dom had donned his jacket once more, flicking his collar right up, and took Kiddo for a walk to a classy teppanyaki grill restaurant.

Tiny: can Raze date me next? I'm salivating.

Trix: you an◦ Quicklips take a quick lunch break. We're sche◦-ule◦ to alternate while they're here.

Kiddo and Dom were seated in a booth, the heat pouring off the grill already as Dom ordered them some dishes in Japanese.

"Who knew that a bowl of salted pod beans could taste like heaven?" Kiddo groaned.

"They sure make you thirsty though," Dom answered with narrowed eyes. His attention had honed in on a table of business people. Or one business woman in particular.

"You recognise her?" Kiddo asked.

"Believe so," Dom nodded. "She might be able to spread the word a little more. Another useful father situation. Be right back with our water."

Dom rose, selecting a stoppered bottle of water for their table from the bar.

On the way back he paused in front of the business luncheon, leaning the glass bottle on their bench. His hand was on the bottle neck, right in front of the woman's nose.

The woman's eyes fell to the lotus on Dom's finger, and then flashed hurriedly up to his face.

Dom spoke to them cheerfully for a moment, gesturing to the street beyond, and then thanked them in Japanese.

"What did you chat about?" Kiddo asked curiously.

Dom was unphased as the business woman rose and excused herself from the table. Hurrying past Dom as if he might spit poison at her.

"I asked them for directions to our drinking alley later on,"

Dom smiled and thanked the chef as the grill hissed with an array of meats being scraped onto it.

"The alley you know very well?"

"That's the one. I also double checked if my particular bar choice and time sounded like a good idea."

"Well done. Hopefully it helps. I'm actually surprised it's taking us so long to find a snatcher who knows of or is in The Hunt."

Dom agreed. "Maybe yesterday's incident was just extremely unlucky," he commented doubtfully, expertly using his chopsticks to fill bowls for both of them. "But now we've got two gossips with connected, dodgy dads on board. I think Blabs will be our real ticket, but it's good to have this lady as back up."

"I'm sure you'll lure us out a good one. It feels like you know everyone," Kiddo awkwardly mashed some meat between his own chopsticks, then accidentally flipped the meat between them so that it flopped back down into the bowl.

"Remember I'm choosing very specific locations, where I know I might have some success," Dom said, eyeing Kiddo's progress with amusement. "You're not going to starve while we're here are you?"

He leaned forward, careful of the heat, and rearranged Kiddo's fingers on the chopsticks.

"I've got this," Kiddo said confidently. And managed to get a tiny sliver of meat into his mouth.

"Oh God," Dom snickered. "My boyfriend's going to starve. My future chef boyfriend. Will starve."

Pash: Quicklips, you make eating sushi look like the harⅾest thing in the worlⅾ.

Velvet: ⅾon't ⅾisrupt him. This is fun to watch.

Quicklips: there's rice in my lap.

Pash: you also just got sauce ⅾown your front.

Kiddo snorted at his phone. "It's not just me having food issues. Thank my lucky stars I'm off washing duty."

"Yes, washing is firmly off your itinerary," Dom asserted. "You seem much more relaxed about all that when you're not at home."

Dom was enjoying himself, having already easily taken three mouthfuls compared to Kiddo's meat sliver.

"Not that this mission is a holiday," Kiddo remarked. "But I don't feel a scrambled need to get every single daily thing done in one go, forgetting half of them in the rush, when I'm not in my usual life."

"Huh," Dom said with interest. "I wonder why it's worse at home."

Another strip of meat squished out from Kiddo's chopsticks before he could get it to his mouth, and Dom kept a studiously blank face.

"Everyone's different. But trying to feel successful at normal life puts me in a bit of a vicious cycle," Kiddo explained.

Dom frowned in thought. "For the record, I like that you're not 'normal', because neither am I. And also because it means you're always absorbed in what actually interests you. Such as cooking, and such as *myself*. But tell me about the cycle."

Kiddo felt his lips pull with a coy smile of gratitude. "Well,

I needed to develop coping strategies when Hato took me in. Hato scheduling my time and responsibilities helped me to get more on track, back when I could barely remember to eat at regular intervals let alone take medication or go to bed. And Flip and the others would train and exercise with me so much that I had way less restless energy to be impulsive with."

"But the trouble now is …?" Dom asked.

"I clung so hard to the jobs I could achieve, like pulling my weight around the warehouse, that I got a bit compulsive. Now I feel overwhelmed and claustrophobic if anything is out of place. And there are heaps of people in our house, moving or marking or messing things all the time," Kiddo felt tired just thinking about it. "When I see one thing that needs doing, I suddenly notice them all, and either can't face them, or try to tackle them all at once." Kiddo blew upward at his fringe in annoyance at it all. "It's such an effort to actually get started on any job, and I do need to do these things to function as a human being, but the moment something's out of place I feel like I'm already on the way to needing to start again."

"Ugh," Dom pulled a face, imagining it. "I hardly notice things like that. How exhausting."

"But, on the upside," Kiddo assured him, "things like my chopstick issues right now would have had me right pissed off when I was young. And I was so jumpy and withdrawn that I wouldn't have said any of this to you, and so inattentive that you would have thought I could hardly care less about you, rather than us enjoying a date day like no other."

Dom leaned his cheeks in his hands, adorably chuffed.

The young blue eyed man in front of Kiddo, listening with such care, was at total odds with the Raze that the business woman had skirted around earlier.

"Anyway, being away from the usual environment has been the right mix of things for me. A combination of well-planned events, and reacting quickly to urgent moments," Kiddo ended on a positive. "Which all suits me to a tee."

Tiny: I ⬧on't like wasabi. I ma⬧e a big mistake.

Velvet: let's hope it's more tolerant of you than you are of it. Start ⬧i⬧n't factor in heaps of toilet stops.

"Here's an idea. Let's live off Hato's budget and go on permanent holidays," Dom suggested. "He would do anything for your health."

"We'll run it by him," Kiddo grinned.

Pash: gaw⬧, Quicklips, just put the sushi ⬧own an⬧ try a ⬧umpling. I want to get a break at some point too.

| 14 |

Fourteen

"Shouldn't have –" thump "–eaten that much." Pash smashed a snatcher in her throat so that she went weak at the knees and dropped her weapon, rather than carrying out her plan to jab Kiddo with a utility knife.

"Keep hold of that one," Trix told Pash – having just slid her sharp geisha styled hair pin through the gullet of another ne'er-do-well.

Kiddo grabbed hold of an old, low hanging balcony – crunching abs and lifting to boot a snatcher hard in the back. Dom stepped aside so that the snatcher went wheeling past himself for a head on collision into the alley's brick wall.

A final snatcher tried to escape down the lane, but Tiny was leaning casually in one entrance, and Quicklips was filling up the other escape. The snatcher got up close and personal with Quicklips' fist and fell like a building under demolition.

"Velvet can't see any others around," Trix reported. "She has a good view from the rooftop."

The female, writhing like a snake in Pash's headlock,

stared at Dom, Trix and Kiddo as they closed in. Her eyes were bulging and wild.

"Don't scream honey," Pash warned against the snatcher's ear. "Your windpipe won't be in top shape right now."

"You ... lured *us* here?" the snatcher rasped, and swallowed with an effort. She seemed genuinely incredulous that snatchers had been jumped. "You were *playing* the lost lamb," she spat at Dom – insulted.

She and her group had fallen for it when the team had decided to try just about anything on the way to their final stop. Picking fights with shady types, or letting Dom wander around 'alone' to try to attract snatchers from the woodworks.

"We were kinda hoping you were after our friend here for an actual, intelligent reason, lovey," Pash purred. "We'll be as disappointed as you if you didn't Hunt him down on purpose."

The snatcher tried to claw Pash's arm and to lash around behind herself. But she yelped when her knuckles cracked against Pash's armour.

"Breasts like steel, darlin," Pash informed her. "Now, why don't you tell us a little about yourself?"

"You're not a local from here, are you?" Dom asked curiously.

The snatcher pursed her lips and darted her eyes away, sweat on her brow.

"Piss off," she hissed thickly. Her throat sounded raw after Pash's hit. "You're dead. All of you." Somehow, it sounded like she meant it, even in her position.

"You're not New Zealander are you?" Dom groaned. "I hate remembering that even the nicest populations have a rotten bunch."

"Did you follow him because you're part of The Hunt?" Trix questioned. She was checking the girl's pockets and backpack for a calling card.

The girl couldn't help but hesitate at the mention of that name.

"She doesn't really fit the bill for 'elite'," Pash frowned, and the girl bared her teeth in fury.

"I'm here to find them," she spat. "When I find them, I'll join them, and make you suffer."

"Your little posse were so easy to trick," Pash tutted. "Why would they want you?"

The girl snarled.

"No calling cards," Trix affirmed. "These guys were a waste of time."

"I bet you didn't even know you were picking a fight with the very people The Hunt most want dead," Pash teased. "We used this specific lost lamb for a reason."

"Hi, I'm Raze," Dom introduced himself politely.

The girl went berserk, thrashing backward.

Kiddo saw her dip her hand down her top and whip something out from her bra.

He saw her push up the blade of a knife, and ram it towards Pash's eye.

Kiddo launched forward to grab the girl's wrist, and all he could do in that instant was swerve her aim so that she squelched the blade into the side of her own neck.

That ended that conversation.

"Yuck," Pash crinkled her nose and dropped the girl. "And thanks."

"Necks and throats are the Raze gang specialty," Dom mused.

Pash grabbed a bottle of sanitiser from her purse. "Did I get mussed up?" she asked worriedly.

"It's actually amazing," Trix shook her head at Pash. "Your lipstick's still intact since this morning."

"And on my break I even ordered spaghetti Bolognese from a machine with pictures and buttons," Pash gushed happily. "Didn't smudge, or make half the mess that Quicklips did."

"Velvet's lipstick," Kiddo reminded them mildly.

Tiny: Why is it taking so long to find someone in the know?

He was still leaning nonchalantly in the laneway entrance, apparently ignoring what was going on in the dark behind him.

Velvet: we need the right snatcher. Not just the ordinary sort.

Quicklips: it's even harder when they're unmasked. Could just be regular pickpockets and low lives, even if they're rare here.

"Lucky Miss Lotus has had a word to the police on our behalf," Trix winced at the mess in the alley. "We've been terrible guests in this city. They deserve the warning."

Velvet: let's move on. I'm done with this perch.

Pash: but you would make the prettiest gargoyle up there.

Kiddo couldn't help but grin as Pash giggled at herself. She had probably been giggling at her messages to the chat all day.

"Our specific targets, Blabs and our business woman, were always going to be our best bet in such a big city," Dom said.

"If they spread the word about the bar tonight, at least one right person is bound to show up there."

"Right," Trix nodded resolutely. "Let's hope. For Seethe's sake."

Velvet: hurry it up. We're all clear.

Trix: Tiny an• Quicklips, you hea• off first.

"And you leave from the opposite side," Trix instructed Pash next, heading out the alley now herself.

Pash gave Dom and Kiddo a sultry wink. "See ya."

Dom pulled Kiddo's hand into his leather jacket pocket to warm up their fingers together.

It was getting cool and dusk had nearly faded to night, with the city's lights and colours coming to life.

"Wait 'til I show you Godzilla," Dom told him. "He's clawing up a cinema on the way to our bar."

"Can't wait," Kiddo squeezed his hand, amazed at how quickly they switched from sightseeing sweethearts, to vengeful Razes and back.

| 15 |

Fifteen

Kiddo was warm in Dom's jacket again, and Dom's sleeves were rolled right up.

The barkeep had started to turn Dom away with a frown when they'd first climbed the steep ladder steps up to the small, dark establishment.

Then the man had seen, even in the dim red light, exactly what style of lotus Dom was wearing.

The barkeep's whole face had brightened with genuine gladness and welcome, ushering them both in.

Two patrons had promptly upped and left, others had clapped Dom on the back. One appeared to start sweating with nerves, quickly facing away. The others were blissfully unaware irregulars or tourists.

Dom had explained that, though this place maxed out at fifteen people, it was one of the larger bars in the area. Large enough for a guest to blend in if needed, and small enough to stand out if needed.

Kiddo assumed that anybody who greeted Dom enthusiastically was lucky enough to have spent some time with him, or even possibly knew what he did for their streets. The others must have also had a reason to outright leave or huddle over their beers.

Kiddo didn't mind so much that he could hardly keep up with the fawning conversations of smitten people surrounding Dom this time, because it gave Kid a chance to step back and observe.

The gang had had to stick to the outside. They were hidden down tight lanes and narrow alleyways. So Kiddo was keeping his eyes peeled, leaning in a corner and keeping out of the way while Dom did his thing.

They all had to be careful for this part of the itinerary. The buzzing, teeming nightlife in this network of famous alleys, with tourists and locals alike squeezing past and weaving along each tight trail, could be a perfect spot for incognito snatchers from around the world, here on 'the hunt'. A quick knifing, a drugged Raze gang member and some nimble Hunters, and it would be that easy for them to be one more team member down.

Quicklips: yo, Velvet. Switch?

Velvet: omw.

The gang were all circulating the confined lanes, and taking turns to roam up and down the normal connecting roads outside, where trouble might spring from. It was going to be hard to slip away if word had actually spread too far, and something organised had been set up.

Tiny: Pash, keep letting people line up to take your picture. It's clearing out my lane.

Pash: what a nice relief for you.

Kiddo heard a pause in the chatter around Dom, like a stutter or intake of breath, as a man in an immaculate suit swept into the snug space.

A white cashmere scarf sat neatly under the lapels of his jacket, and he wore white gloves and a pocket square, as if he was due at the theatre instead of a bar.

He clapped eyes on Dom immediately, and gave a curt nod to the barkeep to get him a beer. The barkeep's smile had been replaced with a solemn expression.

Dom wrapped up his conversations, keeping up his own easy smile, and moved away from the people that Kiddo had decided must be good ones. Dom came to lean back against the bar, his elbows on the counter. He'd put himself in position so that the newcomer was between himself and the unnoticed Kiddo.

"I invited Blabs, but he sent his daddy?" Dom shook his head in disappointment.

"How's Ryo?" the man inquired with a straight face. He sipped his beer and wiped the foam from his lips with a napkin. He hadn't taken off his white gloves – as if concerned the place and its people might be dirty.

"Great. No thanks to you or your brat," Dom's smile was still in place, but it had become sinister.

"It was all in the name of good business," the man stated. "There's always a risk in grabbing someone."

"The risk was also to your own son," Dom snarled. "You had to know we might survive and that I would come looking for the one who set us up."

"My son was a brilliant boy," the man hissed angrily. "Before you did that … that thing to his neck. Now all he can do is usher foreigners onto rides."

"He was never brilliant even before he had a few too many minutes with his air cut off," Dom snorted. "He was stupid enough to think the two of you could be amateur snatchers and hand us in for a profit."

"Well," the man drew a breath to calm himself. "I'm not so amateur anymore."

Dom turned to face the bar, drawing himself closer to the man. "Glad to hear it. I hope you have the most elite contacts your money can buy."

The man drew a cream coloured business card from behind his jacket pocket square. There was a shiny silver wolf's head printed on that card. He handled it delicately in his gloves, as if it was precious.

"Nice," Dom encouraged. "Get out your phone. Bring them here."

The man shook his head. "I shouldn't be surprised that you are as cocky as ever. And, why would I not *already* have them surrounding this place and cutting you off?"

Dom laughed, rubbing his jaw. "For the same reason that I'm not surprised you came directly yourself. Alone. You wanted to see if you alone could manage it. If you could steal the full glory for taking me down."

The man's eyes narrowed. "And how would I dare presume to do that?"

Blabs' father scoffed and played a cool game on the outside, but Kiddo noticed he constantly toyed with the sleeves of his jacket and then adjusted the buttons at the wrists of his gloves. A tell for nerves.

"I'm guessing you would presume to do that by … having a small weapon concealed somewhere," Dom tapped his chin thoughtfully. "And I'm guessing that you wanted to get me close by making me angry. I mean, really, that opening line about Ryo. Hopefully you're fancy enough to have a letter opener or something – not a Stanley knife."

The man tugged at his sleeve again.

Kiddo could bet there was a nasty little knife sheathed up there.

"You'd swipe me, nothing fatal, so I could limp myself out of here without you being reported to the police," Dom went on. "But then you'd find me on my lonesome and I'd be a goner. Is that it? Cash for kills? The Hunt sounds more like an assassin agency than an offshoot of the people hustler biz."

"You think they'll pay me for handing over your dead body?" the man clicked his tongue. "No. No. No. They don't want you taken *down*. They want you taken *in*." The man was smirking. "They want to really draw out what's going to happen to you and your followers."

The wolf icon on the card in front of him seemed to glow evilly in the red lights of the room.

"They want to make an example of you. You especially."

This time, when the man made a gesture toward his sleeve, Kiddo stepped forward and gripped the man's arm, making him start.

Kiddo shared a glance with Dom, though. Frowning, he shook his head.

He hadn't felt a weapon stashed there.

The man shoved Kiddo's grip away, moving The Hunt's card so that Kiddo wasn't at risk of bumping it. It was now even closer to Dom.

"The snatchers are a business," the man continued coolly, as if he was unruffled. "They're turning your threat into an opportunity. They'll monetise their revenge, and boost buyer confidence all in one go. They'll offer up a collection of Razes, and rent each out to their bidders for as long as possible. I've heard they'll even get customers to register what they want a Raze for, so that it's not until it's the highest bidder's turn that anyone gets to permanently keep or destroy their Raze."

Dom banged a hand against the countertop, and Kiddo noticed that the gloved man's eyes shone when Dom got close to touching the card.

"There are no buyers," Dom growled. "They won't get the money or the crowds they're after."

The man tutted. "Be good. Remember, I brought back-up, and am the one calling the shots here. I can have The Hunt take you down instantly."

Kiddo checked his phone. Still not one word of warning from the team. He rolled his eyes and shook his head imperceptibly at Dom once more.

The man was a liar, and he felt safe in his lie.

He seemed much happier now as he kept bluffing and flexing his imaginary power. "There are not many buyers anymore, no. But the ones who are still there are keener than ever. They come from deeper into the shadows. Not the superficial joy or experimental tinkering type of buyers. They are collectors. And the things they want most now are you."

He set his gloved hand to frame the card on the counter, with its red wolf eyes staring, as if he wanted Dom's attention to keep wandering there.

"The auction for your friend is scheduled for the weekend. But when I give *you* to them … the buying frenzy will be unbelievable. I can't imagine what they'll pay me to hand you over in the first place. And then the painfully drawn out end of your life will begin," he said smugly. "It'll be the least I can do after the way you ruined my son's life. And the way you even tried to lure him out again tonight."

Dom laughed. "You really are doing a good job of antagonising me. But, you think I wanted to lure useless Blabs out? I wanted to lure *you* in. You and your card –" Kiddo quickly caught Dom before he could touch the card.

And Dom caught the pure, shocked fury on the man's face when Dom's fingers were halted to hover so close to the wolf.

Dom raised his eyebrows. "You and your card are going to be our key," he finished.

He reached forward in a friendly way to clasp the man's neck, pinching the tendons that connected his neck to his shoulder.

The man paled. "I'll call for –"

"Oh, you see, I do want to go where you were going to send me. But I want that to happen on my terms," Dom explained. The man held perfectly still as Dom reached with his free hand to slowly, carefully draw what had turned out to be a strategically protective glove off the man's fingers. "So," Dom went on. "I'm going to need you to stop showing it off, and bandying it about as your trick weapon, and just scan your card."

"But …"

"Oh, don't worry, they won't come and find *me* here to be picked up. They'll be bringing you in. Which is all I want from you, really."

"Unlock your phone," Kiddo encouraged. "And scan the card."

The man shakily reached into his jacket, not moving too suddenly or in any way that could jostle Dom's hold. He withdrew his phone and used his fingerprint on the sensor.

The anger radiating off the man was palpable. But he hovered his camera over the wolf emblem, and his screen flashed red for a moment, before it returned to normal. There was no sign that he had just set off a beacon and that The Hunt were now already tracking their way to this bar.

"Thanks so much," Dom cooed. Then he slammed the man's forehead against the counter, and when his head bounced back up, the card was stuck to his forehead.

"Now we'll never know if the card was dipped in something, or if the head trauma got him," Kiddo accused.

"Both?"

Dom was working quickly. While the phone was still unlocked he downloaded an app onto the device that would remain hidden amongst countless others. That was all Jingle would need.

Dom tucked the phone into the man's pocket again.

Kiddo: hi team. Take your exits. It's about to get busy. He handed Dom his jacket.

Pash: thank the Lord. My cheeks can't smile no more.

Trix: go! Everybody!

They would all be disappearing down their carefully mapped out manholes and false waterways. Escaping into Miss Lotus' far reaching underground.

"Good luck Raze," the barkeep called after Kiddo and Dom.

Dom blew him a kiss before they slid their way down the ladder.

They dashed through a narrow alley, single file, with Dom running ahead and reaching back to keep Kiddo's hand in his.

Right as Kiddo spotted their particular manhole, Dom whirled about and pushed Kiddo into a doorway.

Pink cut-out blossoms dangled over their heads, and lanterns hung from glowing signs, bobbing in the rush of air they'd just created.

"What –" Kiddo caught his breath.

Before Dom took it away again, with a kiss that could have knocked over a whole world of snatchers.

"That was the best date-day I've ever been on," Dom told him.

And then he was stooping to lift their manhole cover, and ushering Kiddo in.

"Now let's go keep the other Razes from bumping around and getting lost in the dark."

| 16 |

Sixteen

They had cleaned themselves up and were all now flopped tiredly around one of Miss Lotus' night time fires.

Jingle had hacked the ill-fated man's phone and she and Start were working out if the location he had been taken to was legitimate so they could devise a plan.

Quicklips was snoring in the firelight, a hand on his stomach.

"Ahhh man." Lady Pash was in comfortable grey sweats, and was one false eyelash strip away from being man Pash again. The strip of lashes peeled free bit by bit, pulling at Pash's eyelid in a way that made Kiddo wince.

"I think I have as many blisters after wearing flat trekking boots as I would have if I'd worn heels," Pash groaned. He delicately stuck the lash aside on a log so that it was out of the way, and so that it now looked more like a fluffy black caterpillar. "You know, my phone app says we did thirty thousand steps."

"It wouldn't have been worth wrecking the pumps," Velvet muttered. She patted Pash's head and dragged herself off to bed.

Laine approached the tired group hesitantly. She was wringing her hands.

"I'm so sorry to bother you. But, is it alright if I borrow someone's phone charger?" she asked. "Mine hasn't been working. Just like the Cheapie connection."

"Alriiiight," Tiny managed to roll himself up from the grass. "I think mine's the same as yours." He headed for his tent and his bags, with Laine trailing apprehensively after. "You still struggling to receive or send anything from the den?"

"I've had no luck at all," Laine admitted miserably, dismayed by her continuing misfortune.

Poor thing, Kiddo thought tiredly. She was such a brittle person.

"Hey," Blossom and Ryo stopped by the edge of their glade, on their way from saying goodnight at Miss Lotus' house. Dom had gone with them, but hadn't returned yet.

"Hey," Trix nodded, in a cool 'sup' kind of motion.

"I remember that Raze never had enough clean clothes with him," Ryo said to Kiddo with a smile, crouching down beside where Kiddo was sprawled out on the grass. "Because you've been here a bit longer than the others, I thought I'd check to see if you and Doctor Dean wanted me to clean and press your washing with Raze's tomorrow?"

Kiddo put his arm under his head to cushion it as he gazed up at Ryo with appreciation that was no longer grudgingly doled out. Ryo was just a good guy, even if he had a thing for Dom.

"I would really appreciate that," Kiddo told Ryo. "And to not have to think about that bit of washing myself later has just given me a whole new affinity with you."

Ryo laughed and patted Kiddo's shoulder. "It's settled," he straightened. "I'll collect it all from your room tomorrow. Have a great rest."

"You too," Kiddo told him earnestly, and Ryo nodded his thanks. Then he moved off to check in with the red uniformed guards at the nearest cave entrance.

Kiddo noticed then that Blossom's eyes were still honing in on Trix.

"I like your kanzashi weapon," Blossom complimented Trix's ornamental hairpin accessory, crossing to sit beside her.

Trix's short afro curls had been braided back against her head, with the decorative weapon tucked through her hair so that the sharp edge was hidden.

"It can stab and it's pretty," Trix shrugged. "Perfect for me."

"Perfect," Blossom agreed smoothly. "Want to get a drink sometime?"

The tiredness seemed to have evaporated from Trix's posture.

She cocked an eyebrow. "I could do a drink now."

Blossom settled it. "Then now it is."

And they left.

Pash leaned over and closed Kiddo's hanging jaw with a flick of his fingers under Kiddo's chin.

"One less threat to worry about, huh," Pash snickered, referring to Blossom and her attraction to Dom. Pash laid his head on Kiddo's chest and closed his eyes, happy to sleep on the lawn.

Kiddo was half asleep himself when he felt a second form stretch out next to him on his other side.

He wrapped an arm around Dom sleepily, not opening his eyes.

"You good?" he asked Dom with a yawn.

"Mmm," Dom answered unhurriedly, drawing the sound out. "I'm good right here."

"What did you ..." yawn "...talk to Miss Lotus about?"

"Oh," Dom said in an offhand, but quiet voice. "I confessed my sins. And apologised for Tokyo's sudden snatcher problem. It's all flared up since rumours of my attachment to her and her country were spread."

Dom slipped his hand under Kiddo's shirt to rest it on his stomach, and Kiddo could feel the slight, comforting weight of Dom's fingers splayed across his skin.

"And what did she say?" Kiddo questioned. "Were you absolved?"

Those fingers began to trace light circles that tickled and soothed.

"She said that my attachment to her was worth a great deal, in her books," Dom answered. "And that Tokyo could hold its own against things like this."

Kiddo smiled. "I agree on both counts."

A few moments passed. "She also gave the whole greater good argument," Dom added thoughtfully.

"There's that too."

Dom fidgeted a little, when that was normally Kiddo's job.

"Well, like I told Miss Lotus, I want to tell you what I'm

sure you already know anyway. But seeing as you were very honest about yourself earlier, I should also be very open so you know exactly who you're dating."

Dom's fingers kept tracing and circling.

"I'm sure it doesn't surprise you that I would have killed Blabs' father tonight if we hadn't needed him to be transported in for answers," Dom said. "I always kill someone I know to be directly involved in snatching or slaving. And I *always* sleep just fine knowing that I've taken the law into my own hands to get rid of the monsters. In fact, I'm happy being this way. I'm downright glad to kill a people smuggler, an organ harvester, a slaver, a sex trafficker, in any way I can. So … I might work for the 'greater good', but it's my own version of it, and I am not good myself."

"Then none of us are good," Kiddo whispered. "None of us. And I can accept that." He pressed his arm more firmly around Dom's shoulders. "But, Dom?"

"Mmmm?"

"I promise," Kiddo said sincerely. "You are good. So, *so* good. To me. To all of us. And to the people who would be next to be exploited or hurt if you hadn't stopped the monsters first."

Dom angled up to press a kiss to Kiddo's neck.

"You are the light mark still left on my soul."

| 17 |

Seventeen

"What is that *noise?*" Trix asked Jingle, testy after having had quite the late drink with Blossom.

Jingle retreated from her camera for a moment and closed her door. "Big equipment and furniture for the medical wing is being brought in today. And … Sparks is installing a dishwasher," she explained with relief.

"Seriously?" Dom spluttered incredulously. "It took Kiddo being away for a few days for Hato to commission a dishwasher?" He folded his arms. "I bet you've all been living off cereal and microwave dinners with the cook gone too."

"We do miss you Kiddo," Start whined, up in the library again. "Who knew how many groceries a household and a bunch of trainees could go through?"

"I knew," Kiddo smiled.

Dom was clenching his jaw. "What the hell you guys. You better not expect Kid to keep feeding you like babies during culinary training. He won't have time."

"Actually," Hato was sharing a laptop with Flip on the ground level. "The dishwasher is an acknowledgement that

Kiddo has outgrown certain things. Soon he'll have new, bigger responsibilities and routines of his own, other than household chores."

"Exciting stuff," Kiddo told the gang with lack lustre enthusiasm. He nudged Dom with his elbow. "But if the course doesn't work out, I could always be the dishwasher loader to pull my weight."

"No, no," Flip negated. "You're already a busy Razer too, and about to be busier with those studies," Flip supplied. "We'll just have to rescue a replacement butler."

Dom growled, but leaned back moodily against the concrete wall, arms still crossed.

Kiddo heard Laine also make an impatient 'tsk' sound beside him. They'd brought the poor woman with them this morning, considering she would be able to stay right there in the shelter of the tunnel with the laptop – and hopefully be waiting to comfort Seethe if all went well.

But being so close to their goal, Kiddo could tell that her anxiety and agitation were growing with each moment. She was chewing at her bottom lip and holding her purse to herself defensively.

The purse was her comfort right now. In her frightened state, she had asked for a small handgun to keep in there in case things got dangerous down in the tunnels.

It was understandable, after having come in contact with snatchers twice in a week, so Quicklips had taken pity on her. He'd asked to borrow one of the red uniformed guards' weapons for her – having put the safety on very firmly and showing her how to make sure it stayed on.

Kiddo hated to think how dire things would need to have

become, if their last hope was little Laine and her shaking gun.

"It's alright," Kiddo told her softly. "We're just waiting for Start's file. He's sending it to everyone now. And hey," he brightened. "At least your Cheapies phone reception should be working at this level, out of the den."

She nodded, trying for a weak smile. But she had been out of sorts with nerves since before they had left, and would of course continue to be until Seethe was free.

That morning Dom had guided them through the tunnel networks to this exact spot, which Start had specifically marked out for them. Because, above their heads, was the luxury business and apartment tower currently being used by The Hunt.

Quicklips, Trix, Pash, Kiddo and Dom were underground with Laine, and would be taking on the building above. Velvet and Tiny, on the other hand, had joined through the screen chat. They were seated at a café across the road, sipping drinks and ready for an emergency. They would keep rotating close-by hospitality establishments and sampling the goods to perform their duty to the group today.

Velvet slowly licking hot chocolate foam from a teaspoon, and Tiny tucking into a sashimi roll really highlighted how seriously they were taking their jobs.

"Alright," Trix told Start, glancing at the document on her phone. "We're all on."

"Perfect," Start said, and the screen light reflected off his glasses as he pulled up some blueprints to share on the laptop. "I'm showing you the detailed version now. But for the heat of the moment, you all have a file with the simplified version of the building's layout for a map. I've marked every entry or exit point. Now that you've loaded this file, it's a live document that you can access at any time and that I can update as the situation changes."

"It's getting more and more important that I don't drop my phone," Pash reflected, straightening a black bandana she had tied about her neck. "Apart from all my selfies."

"If you do drop it, they won't be able to crack it," Jingle promised. "But you'll be lost until you can get to wi-fi."

"And if I drop it, it'll be tragically cracked and I'll be sadly lost in other ways," Pash asserted, now smoothing her sleek black bob.

"The one phone I want to get my hands on now is Doctor Dean's," Jingle added, making Laine blanche with surprise.

"W-why?"

Jingle smirked. "To get you off that damn Cheapies. And because you have Seethe and Hato's numbers, on an unprotected device."

"Yes, yes, keep hold of your tech," Start cut in, wanting the attention back on his map. "You'll notice here that the third level seems the most likely spot to hold a prisoner, as well as an auction," he commented, circling that part of the blueprint. "It has some glass wall office spaces on the far side, but is otherwise a big open level for collaborative work, with polished concrete render, according to the website. The building is brand new, and no company has yet made their home in it, so the site's images of the space being largely empty can probably still be trusted, and mean that they could easily host an event for a number of people in there."

"Looks like small living spaces on the higher levels," Tiny

commented around a mouthful. "And more offices and communal areas below."

"A heli-pad and a pool on top," Velvet added, sizing up the real estate with interest. "Perhaps we could add a rooftop pool while we're doing dishwashers and warehouse extensions at home."

"Firstly," Start ploughed on with his plan. "The building is so new and empty that its elevators and security cameras aren't hooked up yet. Which means we are going to need the very best of us at sneaking to scope out exactly what it's like inside, and to confirm Seethe's location."

"That would be me," Dom volunteered. "Number one chute shuffler. And brand new chutes sound like a dream."

Start was nodding. "If you follow the dotted line," Start clicked something, and the simplified map they all had open on their phones suddenly updated. It now showed a bright purple trail that apparently moved between the layers dividing the building's levels. "You have the greatest chance of getting to the third level and finding Seethe. You won't have to keep checking your phone though – I'll track your device and call out directions."

"Please don't call out," Dom said. "Be very quiet. Number one chute shuffler rule."

Trix opened a headphones case then, and pulled out a hands-free earpiece and something similar to a bendy, wire pipe cleaner.

She hooked the ear piece around Dom's ear, but then firmly pressed the bendy wire into his hand. "Do not drag this around carelessly. It's flexible, but it's a very delicate camera.

It has incredibly sensitive audio recording capability, so that you can take us along for the ride with you."

"Ok," he assured her. "I'll be careful." He twisted the wire around his other ear like a second ear piece – carefully.

"These are also cameras," Trix went on, lifting a plastic strip of see through dots, which simply looked like small craft adhesives. "Stick them anywhere you can to get us eyes inside. And you need to –"

"Be careful?" Dom asked.

"Because they are so new that Jingle's military contacts haven't even used them in the field yet."

"New chutes and new tech," Dom nodded the affirmative. "Careful, careful."

"Once Dom finds his way to Seethe, it'll be up to Dom to smuggle Seethe back out again through the walls and floors," Start announced. "And the rest of you will step up only then. Accidentally drawing attention and putting The Hunt on alert too early could be fatal."

"Everyone else, find where Start has initialled your name on the map," Jingle instructed. "That'll be where you'll surface from."

Quicklips zoomed in and scrolled around the map. "Nice work, there'll be Razes randomly popping out of broom cupboards, parking bays and pipes all over the first level. That'll confuse the socks off 'em."

"It seems Miss Lotus is especially attentive at establishing her routes into new buildings," Start nodded. "Which is very lucky for us. And kind of scary for Tokyo."

"Good luck Dominic," Hato said gravely then. "We'll be watching and listening along with you."

"And keeping very quiet," Dom warned, waving his lotus tattooed finger.

"Bring him back," Laine stepped toward Dom as he pushed off from the wall and shrugged out of his jacket. "Bring him back to me," she gripped the material of his t-shirt desperately.

"Yes ma'am," he told her seriously.

"Ooooh, me, me," Pash gushed, taking Dom's jacket before he could set it down. Pash happily pulled it over her voluptuous vest-chest. "So spunky."

"Indeed," Dom grinned. He in turn loosened the bandana from around Pash's neck, pulling it free.

Then he turned to press his lips to Kiddo's in farewell, and tied the black material over his mouth and nose.

| 18 |

Eighteen

"You have a lovely radio voice," Dom breathed to Start.

The hands-free and camera were so sensitive that they could hear the faint swish of his movements, his light, paced breathing, and even the smallest whisper uttered from his bandana muffled lips.

The endless vision of passing, claustrophobic industrial chute walls – dusty, albeit new, had already got Kiddo completely lost. Nevertheless, they were all breathlessly watching as his footage was shared over the video call.

Tiny and Velvet, now muted and in a new café, had even paused their dining experience to watch.

"Left and up," Start murmured in return.

Up sounded easier than it was.

Kiddo was chewing his knuckles as Dom somehow managed to near silently worm and pull himself upward. He eased himself past bulges in the sheets of metal, trying to limit the noise of his shifting weight by counting on the carefully placed soles of his shoes, his slowly placed knees, and the slight purchase that his elbows, palms and finger pads could offer him for grips.

As if the pressure of the climb or forward wriggling was not an agonising enough feat, whenever Dom passed an air vent he would slip the camera around his ear free and poke it out to give them a better idea of the set-up. Then he would stick a mini adhesive lens onto the vent frame for Jingle to activate.

As Start had thought, the first two levels were designated for more independent offices and break rooms. Beyond a modern set up of many executive style desks and a number of partitions, the levels hadn't been moved into for use yet, and they didn't have Seethe in them.

There were a few people in vests – Hunters, moving about the halls like security, but it seemed likely that everyone else was up in the living levels.

"Did that guy just have …" Quicklips frowned after Dom withdrew from another vent.

"Sharpened teeth," Laine whispered.

Laine was gripping her purse tightly with anxiety as Dom lithely followed Start's guidance upward and to the left again, so that he would arrive over the small glass offices on the empty and open plan third level.

Pash had the fingers on both hands crossed, watching Dom draw nearer to the light of an air vent ahead.

And then Dom and the movement of the footage froze.

Kiddo sucked in a breath.

Dom had heard something.

A door opening?

It had been a faint clang.

Glass screening?

Everyone else strained to hear it too.

"One of your keenest bidders is here," someone said. "He says he's missed you!"

"How many others are here?" a brusque interjection from a second voice.

"Oh, you are one of the first, but we expect more to be flying in tonight to make use of our rooms."

There was a sharp slapping sound. "Head up, animal," the salesy sounding voice said. "Let's see that face."

Dom was on the move again – quick but cautious, easing his way to the vent.

"Well holy shit," the brusque voice uttered. "It *is* him. When I saw the advert photo, and it said this one was part of the Raze gang – even if not the original Raze ..." Dom manoeuvred the camera to catch a man shaking his head in wonder. "I had to see him for myself."

The sly faced, wiry man, wearing a vest and with his side to the camera, reeked of snatcher. Or Hunter. But the other one was bulky, broad and, while well dressed, gave off a dangerous gangster vibe.

Hato started to swear, and Flip quickly muted their end.

Kiddo saw Hato's lips move though. And the message was still loud and clear.

... Our owner...

Kiddo felt the blood drain from his face.

One of Seethe and Hato's past owners?

A drug lord?

The front wall and door of the small office were made of

thick glass. But the others were rendered, with the back wall having had thick, steel loops screwed into the concrete.

Seethe was chained to the back wall like a zoo creature – strung up and contained so that high paying customers could get the up close experience. Strands of ash blonde hair were falling over his face, which seemed unmarked for the buyer's pleasure, but unwell.

He'd been stripped down to a singlet and jeans, with even his feet bare. And Kiddo wondered if they'd fed him in the days since he'd been taken. Surely not feeding him was a bad idea for sales? He was already a lean person, more inclined to shed weight than gain it.

Seethe was breathing heavily, his arms trussed up over his head so that his body was stretched and did seem thinner than ever. Gaunt. But his eyes were as dangerous as ever too.

"Mute us too," Quicklips mouthed to Trix, when Laine couldn't stifle her ragged gasps for air. Trix nodded, and did so with a grim face.

"Don't you recognise me?" the drug baron asked. "I got you off the streets when you were just a kid."

His shoulders heaving with hate, Seethe suddenly hucked from the back of his throat, and shot a bullet of saliva at the two men.

He gave them that piece of himself with such venom, it was a wonder the spit didn't turn to acid and burn through the Hunter's enraged face – where it had hit him on the cheek and mouth.

The baron smirked. He reached into his jacket and handed the Hunter a handkerchief.

Disgusted, the Hunter wiped his face, and bared sharpened canine teeth.

"You *do* remember," Seethe's old master said to Seethe. "I couldn't forget you either. Not after I saw your friend's true value. Not after I had to honour our crazy bargain. It was an intolerable loss."

"How could I forget that face?" Seethe hissed back at last. "It's imprinted into my brain. Like an ugly internal branding."

"Ugly?"

Seethe swore and glared. "Hideous."

The baron stepped closer to Seethe then, observing him closely.

"Have you been doing what I asked?" the baron questioned the Hunter.

The Hunter shrugged silkily. "Every morning and night. I hid the bruises between his toes. But my stock and your incentive ran out this morning I'm afraid."

Kiddo shared a horrified glance with the gang members. Sure he knew what that meant.

The baron reached inside his jacket for the breast pocket again. He pulled out a small plastic bag. A seemingly innocent square filled with delicate white powder.

"Hold his jaw," he instructed the Hunter.

The Hunter folded his arms, his lip curling and exposing that overly pointed canine tooth once more.

"I'm afraid any further fun has to be paid for. You'll need to register your wishes and bid for your time with him. Rest assured, we'll carefully work out the order of people he'll be loaned out to, so that he's not ruined for the final bidder."

The drug lord was unmoved. "I am going to buy out all of his time slots, and be his final bidder too. Then I'll pour even more money into your organisation when you get the big one I also used to own. Neither of them are the original Raze, but that's not what I want them for."

"I need some further reassurance," the Hunter wavered. "Another guarantee."

"I will give my collateral to you personally, if you are the one who keeps working with me on this."

The Hunter was considering – so close to the brink of reverting back to typical, selfish, easily corrupted snatcher status.

"I just want to settle him down so we can have a better chat." The baron tilted his head, as if wondering what the problem was.

The Hunter's crossed arms dropped. He came forward and grabbed Seethe's head as Seethe tried to writhe to get out of the way. In a harsh lock around Seethe's face, the Hunter risked Seethe's gnashing teeth and managed to pry his jaws open.

Laine was whimpering, and Kiddo put his arm around her.

She watched the screen as the baron dipped a finger into the white powder.

He rubbed it on Seethe's teeth.

"It'll be ok," Kiddo tried to calm her. Her fingers were clawing into the sides of her bag as if it were a stress ball. "Seethe can come back from that."

"It took him *years* to break free of the drugs they'd pumped into him when he was first snatched," she howled.

"Careful of that gun in there," Quicklips reminded her, wincing at her purse.

"What they've just given him isn't the worst kind of stuff," Kiddo promised. "He won't get hooked on that."

Kid didn't want to mention what else the baron's ally could have been doing to Seethe every morning and night.

"Give us some time together," the baron said then.

The Hunter scowled at Seethe as he released his head. Seeming animalistic himself, the Hunter bared his teeth and wiped his hands as if he had touched something filthy.

Both canines were certainly unnaturally sharp. Filed to wolf-like points.

"I'm afraid that would be going too far. He is our first Raze, and while he clearly means something different to you than he does to us, he still means a lot."

The baron reached back into his jacket pocket again. He withdrew a neat roll of cash. "Give us some time together," he repeated. "Here's my collateral to prove that I intend to own him, and the rest of his time for the rest of his days."

The colour of the notes and the number of zeroes curving visibly on just the top note of that one pocket roll definitely proved the baron was serious.

"He is quite priceless," the Hunter said flatly. "He is our only hope of luring in the true Raze, as soon as tomorrow. I would be remiss to leave him unattended."

"I have another roll waiting in this pocket as a thank you when I finish my visit," the baron smiled smoothly.

The Hunter pursed his lips. And then he truly was just a snatcher again – filed sharp teeth and all. He put on a charming smile of his own, taking the proffered roll of notes.

"Come and join everyone upstairs when you're done. Yorak will want to welcome you."

The snatcher left the glass walled office, crossed the echoing open space, and closed the door to the room firmly behind himself.

"Why is he doing this to Seethe?" Laine moaned.

Kiddo rubbed her shoulders absently, caught by the horror of the scene.

The camera was shaking slightly in Dom's hold.

"You hardly ever dealt with us yourself. But you sure must've got a strong impression from us," Seethe snarled. "I feel special."

The baron gave a slight smile, though it was more real than what he had so far given the snatcher.

"You and your friend have been the one black mark against my reputation for years," he answered. "I stopped being a joke for it a long time ago. But the mark was still there, nagging away at me for all this time."

Seethe lifted his head enough to glare. "You weren't even the one who really owned us. Those thugs in the lab were our buyers."

"I owned those thugs. I own that world. And I ran that fateful gladiator bout to entertain so many of my peers."

"Fine," Seethe sank back against the concrete wall. "Why'd you wait then? You were too long. My friend is dead."

Hato, muted and gripping Flip's arm for support, was very much not dead.

The baron was reaching into that jacket pocket again, for a fourth time.

"Liar. Of course you are. But I *know*. You were both doing so well for yourselves because of that bargain, running your nightclub. You were the ones who got away, but I had made a public bet and couldn't go back on it."

He withdrew a rolled up cloth case from the pocket. The kind that might contain discrete torture knives or –

"Against the odds, I lost the bargain. But I didn't want to lose face too. How would I look as a businessman if I went back on my word?"

"You're a kingpin," Seethe cackled. "You would have looked just as dirty as your clientele expects. And you would have stopped being a joke much sooner."

Seethe's old master tutted. "Even *you* know there is a type of 'honour among thieves'. I could not tarnish my trustworthy name."

"Oh lawd," Seethe gagged, dripping disbelief.

"But now the whole underworld specifically hates you and your dear *Hato*," the drug lord went on. "Nobody would say a word about me going after you again."

He crouched down and unrolled the cloth wrap on the smooth concrete floor.

Kiddo swore.

"It was too perfect, the sublime moment I saw your picture and realised what you had become. A Raze," the baron chuckled. "My addict, with such a noble cause."

The roll contained a line of syringes, each already set in its own cylindrical case with a dose of something nasty waiting to be injected into a reformed user.

"I got clean as soon as your lot weren't there to pump me full of their spoiled stuff," Seethe said, sickly.

"Not as soon as you were free, I bet," Seethe's master disagreed. "And you might not have been a user for a while, but do you ever really stop being an addict? I mean, I'm sure you can't honestly tell me you haven't enjoyed what my little ally has been giving you for the last few days."

He selected one of the syringes and started unpackaging it.

"But I brought you much stronger stuff for today onwards."

Laine was shaking her head over and over, back and forth. Hato's cheeks had tears on them.

"Dom, do not move." Start's voice was as unsteady as the camera Dom held. "Do not move. He's in no shape to get out of there if this man raises an alarm. Seethe needs to be able to take his time."

"Just wait," Jingle pleaded as quietly and with as much tension. "Wait until you can avoid making any noise. The others will be there when the time is right, and you'll be able to make it no matter how sick he is."

"We can bring him back from this," Start whispered hoarsely. "If you wait until this man is done, Dom, we can save Seethe for sure."

"You still have that junkie body. And that junkie fire," the man went on. "The Seethe I owned is just waiting under the surface for me to bring him back."

The syringe laid ready. The baron tugged a rubber cord

free from a pouch in the roll of cloth. He stood to face Seethe again.

"All that blood has drained from your arms," the baron sighed. "We'll have to get a good pool happening. I don't like touching too many other places myself, you see. And I obviously don't mind if other buyers see the marks on you and decide not to bid."

Kiddo was rhythmically rubbing Laine's shoulders. But it wasn't helping either of them.

"Wait Dom. Just wait."

The baron tied the cord tightly around Seethe's arm. Soon a vein would be bulging there.

"Why would you waste your money and your product on me?" Seethe growled. "Just slit my throat and move on."

"Waste?" the baron tilted his head, as if surprised. "I was never sure I would get my chance with you at all. But now, I'll be here with you every chance I get." He gestured at the other syringes. "I'll kill you with kindness. Make you my slave. I won't even need to chain you after too long. You'll be a prize in one of my brothels, earning your keep, and counting on me in every way for your next fix."

Seethe's eyes closed and his head hung as, too quickly, it was happening. The baron pricked a throbbing vein, pressed down and let the liquid inject into Seethe.

Then the baron affectionately slapped Seethe's stubbled cheek, and untied the cord.

It felt like no one in the tunnel was breathing as the baron tucked his cloth bundle back into his jacket pocket.

"I'll detox," Seethe promised. "I won't ever be a slave again."

"We'll see," the baron said. "In fact, I'll see you again soon."

And then he was gone.

| 19 |

Nineteen

Dom hardly waited for the door to be closed.

He wedged the camera into the corner of the vent opening and left it.

His movements were fast, though still managed to be deathly silent as he eased the vent cover free and angled it into the chute to rest there.

Then he was deftly dropping on light feet into the office turned cell.

Seethe's face paled further.

He shook his head at the image of Dom.

"I'm seeing things already?" he husked. "The brother I lost."

Dom pulled down Pash's bandanna – his tears having left tracks in the dust on his cheeks. He ghosted toward Seethe and threw his arms around Seethe's lean body in a rush.

"You never lost me," Dom uttered, his voice straining with emotion and the need to be quiet. "I'm right here. We're here. We're going to get you out. The team are just waiting on my word."

In fact, they were getting ready to move to their respective stations at that very moment. Now was the time to create distractions and havoc on level one.

Jingle had signalled that, though limited, her cameras were online. She would let everyone know where to target.

On screen, Dom reached for the cuffs around Seethe's wrists, wincing at a light clanking noise, and then patting at his pockets for a blade or something sharp.

"Don't you dare," Seethe smiled slowly. "Don't you touch those chains. Tell the team not to move."

Dom pulled back. "You're just tripping a bit," he said worriedly. "But I can get you out."

"I *am* tripping," Seethe agreed. "It feels like my pupils are shrinking right down to pinpricks. Last night they were swelling right up to boggle out of my head."

"I'll help you keep steady," Dom promised desperately, he now held a box cutter, probably pilfered from one of their attackers on yesterday's adventures, and he was reaching for the cuffs. "It'll be ok."

"Don't," Seethe repeated adamantly. "Just listen."

Dom paused. Despite the pressure of the moment. Despite Seethe apparently being on his way to an out of body experience. He stopped, putting his hand on Seethe's face, drawing a breath. And he listened.

"I can get through this," Seethe swallowed. "Especially knowing that you are all here."

"You don't hav–"

"I want to stay here, so that they don't know you've found them," Seethe cut him off. "So that all those buyers and as many of these 'Hunters' as possible all come together for their auction tomorrow." He shook his head, as if he couldn't see straight. He was sweating. "And so that I can have a front row seat when you raze them all to hell."

Dom gaped. Wide eyed.

"Give 'em what they want," Seethe glowered. "If they wanted to draw you here to the auction. Then come to the auction."

"No," Laine was gasping. "No, don't you dare leave him."

"If you trust me to get through this," Seethe said through his teeth. "You will leave me, and use this chance to get rid of as many of them as you can. It's just like when you trusted Kiddo to get through the snacher convention."

"Noooo," Laine wailed. She was clawing open her purse. Probably fishing for tissues. But nothing like that would help.

"I promise, we'll find a way to get you. And to get them," Dom was saying.

Start and Jingle were already spouting suggestions in Dom's ear. He should spend some more time going through the chutes above the passageways and stairwells, branching out from there. He should put up as many more cameras as possible.

"I can't accept this," Laine was muttering. "No, no, *no*."

Start was firm. The team must not surface. Nobody should know they'd been there.

Hato was resolute.

Velvet's expression was pinched, but hard.

Dom was hugging Seethe as if he were a dying man in a final embrace.

"No, no, no, no, no," Laine's voice was becoming harsh.

"Hello?" Trix frowned, her face patchy from withheld tears as she answered a new, separate screen call on her phone.

Blossom and Ryo were in Miss Lotus' security rooms, the blue lights illuminating their faces and enhancing their worry.

Kiddo started with surprise when Laine stepped out of his embrace and turned, dropping her purse.

She held something cold and hard to his forehead.

He was at such close range that he could see that the safety Quicklips had ensured was firmly on, was now firmly off.

Kiddo raised his hands.

"This fell out of Doctor Dean's washing," Ryo urgently held up a cream coloured card with a wolf's head logo.

Quicklips gasped.

Pash whirled.

Trix stiffly lowered the phone.

"This is unacceptable Dominic!" Laine yelled at the laptop. "Bring Seethe to me or I will take Kiddo from you!"

She was flinching and shaking so much that her finger was at risk of squeezing the trigger with a nervous jerk.

"Dom can't hear you honey," Pash said slowly. "Threatening Kiddo won't work on him when we're on mute."

"Seethe doesn't know what he's saying! We can't leave him there!" Laine wailed.

With a stony face, Trix closed the laptop before any of the others in the call noticed what was happening and said something to panic Dom.

"Seethe does know exactly what battle he's facing," Quicklips tried to take a step forward, but something in Laine's body language and expression stopped him in his tracks. "We can carry out his plan, and get him back."

"I am not risking Seethe further or wasting any more time before he's sold," she cried. "After my first call failed, you all seemed so promising. Like you could beat them. And I gave you a chance. But then you were so slow, and now refuse to even get him out of this when we're right here, let alone save him from a whole future of this kind of thing!"

"Your first call?" Trix asked in a hard voice.

Laine's nose was running, and she was shuddering. The gun was so close to Kiddo's eyes that he could see how she tightly clutched the grip as if her life depended on it. Her knuckles were white with the effort.

"Didn't you notice how fast they found Dom and Kiddo when they were being careful, but how long it took them to find you all when you were trying?" Laine laughed in an unhappy way, sobbing at the same time. Even she couldn't believe what she was doing. "If you'd taken me along the second time, it would have been much quicker."

"Why didn't you *tell* us that they'd got to you after Seethe was taken?" Quicklips asked. "We could have used the card. We would have understood."

"It didn't work after the first time I scanned it in the cat café restroom," Laine answered wretchedly. "I thought it was useless, so I hid it at the bottom of my dirty wash. But I came to realise that it was my damn Cheapie phone provider that was useless – down in Miss Lotus's den. Just like Tiny's."

She peered down at where her torn open purse now sat at

her feet. Another Hunt card rested, face up, at the top of her bag.

"But it turns out it really was only a problem in the den," Laine said with misery. "The card works further up. It worked just now. Thank God I hid the spare in my purse card holder."

"Guys, get out of here," Kiddo said quickly. "She only needs me."

"Yes. It's fine," she sobbed in agreement. "I don't want to hurt any of you. I'm sure you really do think you're doing your best by Seethe. So go. Kiddo is what will bring Dom, and that will be enough to get me Seethe back."

"Go, so you can save us later!" Kiddo insisted.

"They'll be here any minute," Laine warned hopelessly.

"Hell no," Pash began. She sprang to action to try to rush Laine, leaping into a pounce with arms outstretched.

Laine screamed, and in an instant she had moved the gun.

She pulled the trigger in the middle of the motion, and two people went down.

Kiddo, deafened, and his vision tilting as he clutched at the open rivet that had been scraped along the side of his head.

And Pash, smoking from the chest, and thrown backward into Quicklips.

"GO!" Kiddo roared over the explosions in his head.

It was kind of like a migraine and a seizure had had a love child in there.

"PLEASE!" he yelled at them.

And he was suddenly winded too, as there was a thump on his chest and stomach.

Laine had panicked and jumped straight back on top of

him, pinning him, with the gun quickly held to his sternum. Her face was white as a sheet, and she seemed just like a frightened child, though he couldn't hear the wracking sounds that appeared to be raking free of her body.

His ears were ringing.

Trix and Quicklips were wild-eyed, staring at the gun over Kiddo's heart as if they were caught watching a horror movie.

Then then unfroze.

Trix grabbed the laptop.

Quicklips scooped up the stricken Pash.

And, glancing back at him in fear, they did what Kiddo had asked.

They left.

Disappearing down the tunnels as if The Hunt was on their heels.

But in just a few moments The Hunt was right there, with their sights set on the mess that was Kiddo and Laine instead.

Four of them poured down a manhole a distance away, having finally worked out where in the world Laine's signal had come from, when there was nobody standing on the surface.

Kiddo gritted his teeth, trying to shake his head back into order.

This was worse than unchecked ADHD on drugs, alcohol, puberty and at a party.

The Hunters listened to Laine's demands.

She was gesturing agitatedly with the gun.

They were nodding, agreeing.

They had unnaturally sharpened canine teeth.

One of them was the Hunter who had only just done a deal with the drug baron. He was having quite the busy day.

Laine backed off Kiddo, standing, and the Hunters stooped to yank him up by his arms.

He stood, dizzily, while he was cable tied – his wrists forced together behind his back.

Laine kept moving the gun from them to Kiddo, trying desperately to establish that she was in charge, while becoming increasingly less so with each erratic movement.

Unbothered, the Hunters fell in around Laine and Kiddo, leading them up a ramp in the distance that Kiddo was pretty sure he'd actually been marked down to use if Start's plan had gone ahead.

The baron's ally was eyeing Kiddo as if to work out how much more he might have just been put into a position to personally gain.

Laine stuck close to Kid, almost as if she still wanted him to comfort her even now, and as the ringing in his ears faded, he started to notice the loud drags for breath she was taking.

He really couldn't care, though, as the blood trickled from the itching, stinging trench that had been carved into the side of his scalp.

It hadn't been a life threatening shot, but it was full of heat and was throbbing. It had sploshed red down his cheek, ear, shoulder and arm. Warmly tickling the side of his neck.

And each stair caused a small burst of stars in Kid's eyes.

Their group didn't pass any other Hunters as they climbed the steps, so perhaps these ones had been the ones on duty. They also apparently did exactly what Laine had demanded; marching her and Kiddo straight up to the third floor.

Kiddo wasn't at all relieved to see Seethe face to face when he was led into the very cell that they had all been watching so recently.

Seethe was not happy either. He was not tripping quite enough to be able to mistake the gory sight of Kiddo, his girlfriend holding a wobbly gun, and both of them surrounded by sharp toothed Hunters.

"Oh fu–"

"Alright," Laine gasped at the Hunters. "I won't shoot this one … again …" she swallowed and jabbed the gun toward Kiddo, "… if you unlock Seethe, and give him to me."

"How exactly is 'this one' better as a ticket to the first Raze?" a Hunter queried flatly. She picked at her sharpened canine with an equally sharp fingernail. "I'd say it's best to keep both."

"Kiddo is his boyfriend," Laine stuttered. "Raze would do anything for him. He'll come."

"Oh Laine," Seethe uttered. "No."

"I did it for you Seethe," Laine sobbed hopefully. "I'm going to save you. Not just from this situation, but forever. They promised they'll forget you were ever a Raze. We can live normally if we give them the first Raze in your place!"

Laine's phone started ringing. Well and truly working now that she was above ground.

"Answer it," the baron's ally grinned toothily in delight, seeing the name on the screen. "If you have a direct line to the one called Hato, we might just leave your future children alone too." He played absently with a chest pocket on his vest – probably thinking about how the roll of money in there could be multiplied if he could just nab Hato for the drug lord.

Laine was gaping when Hato's worried face filled the screen. His volume was muted.

"Oh wow," another Hunter chortled. "We've never been able to penetrate the Raze gang techie's firewalls or security. We had no idea where to even start looking." He snatched for Laine's phone. "Hand it over."

"N-no," she turned the gun from Kiddo to the four Hunters. "Free Seethe and let us out."

"So far we've got no original Raze, and no useful phone," the female Hunter mused. "All we've got is a bleeding, if good looking, youth you claim to be Raze's boyfriend."

"Kiddo is one of the Raze gang," Laine added in a rush. "Another Raze."

"Laine, stop," Seethe begged.

"It's all for you," she wept. "It will be alright."

"No," Seethe disagreed vehemently. "The moment you betrayed them, you betrayed me," Seethe told her. "It will never be alright again."

Laine moaned. Her eyes darted from one problem to the next.

"Fascinating," the drug lord's ally stated. He was still watching Hato on Laine's phone. "He looks positively ready to beat his chest."

"Yes, he loves Kiddo too," Laine told them, moving to hold the phone protectively against herself. "You might end up with Kiddo, Hato, and the original Raze in exchange for Seethe!"

"Might?" the female drawled. "Hmmm. Doesn't sound very promising."

Before Laine could whirl on the female Hunter, one of her comrades darted forward.

And just like that, Laine had lost the gun.

| 20 |

Twenty

"We have to tell Yorak that he has a new Raze to auction off," the female Hunter stated lazily. "He can decide about the usefulness of the phone and where to put the new Raze. We're just the first responders."

"I'll report it," another replied eagerly. He crossed the large space and headed out the door purposefully, before any of the other three could volunteer.

"Well, someone's competitive to give Yorak good news," the baron's ally glared after the one who had just left the room. "Such a pleaser."

"We all are, when it comes to Yorak," the grim, sharp toothed male closest Kiddo grunted. He held Laine's gun.

Laine was trembling and leaning from foot to foot between the three Hunters, so hysterical with fear she couldn't decide what to do.

"Shame about his head," the female mused as she observed Kiddo. "He's gorgeous. But a fresh wound like that won't cover up well."

Kiddo stood resolutely, a dark expression on his face and

his chin jutted up. He had planted his feet wide to try to give himself balance and to be as ready as possible for anything.

Laine, on the other hand, now tottered and sank down between Seethe and Kiddo – ringed in, and bunching her hands in her hair and over her ears as if she could block everything out.

"Who knows. If the true Raze actually is this one's boyfriend, we could really be the winners here," the baron's ally shrugged.

"I'd say *I'm* the winner in that scenario," a venomous voice came from the doorway.

Dom dragged the Hunter who had just left the room back in by the vest. His neck lolled loosely.

So Yorak wouldn't be getting his good news.

Dom sent the Hunter's body skidding across the polished concrete floor, and closed the door quietly behind himself. Bolting it from the inside.

Kiddo dove, shouldering the gun toting male before he could aim at Dom.

Dom didn't wait, sprinting across the space – hurtling toward the baron's ally, who had sprung into action. The sly Hunter burst from the office, closing the distance between them.

"Don't kill him," the female cautioned the baron's ally. "I think he's the one!"

Dom and the baron's ally clashed in something between combat and collision. At the same time Kiddo and his opponent went down together in a tangle of limbs.

Kiddo swivelled as best he could and clunked a heavy boot

down on the gun wielder's head, so that there was a crunch against the concrete. He gave one more stomp for good measure.

Laine had squeaked and scrabbled away from the mess, but the female Hunter strode forward.

With a grunt, Kiddo felt himself being torn backwards by the Huntress' grip on his hair. She ripped him off her limp comrade, and in turn seized the gun – plucking it coolly from dead fingers.

Kiddo yelped and arched as he landed awkwardly on his strained arms, but then kicked out at the Huntress' shins before she could threaten anyone.

Snarling, she instinctively whacked him across the cheek with the butt of the gun as she wheeled around, and then cursed at the extra, visible damage she'd done to his aesthetics.

As Kiddo blinked stars against the cold ground, her own eyes darted to Dom's battle with the baron's ally.

Dom was winning.

Which meant in a moment she would be alone.

He saw her ready herself to yell at Dom to stop, to draw Dom's attention to the gun.

And while the gun was quite the threat, Kiddo knew that if she yelled, *that* would seal their fate for sure.

So far nothing too loud, other than grunts, cracks and punches had come from their fight. Nothing to have alerted anyone else upstairs.

The first Hunter hadn't even had a chance to report that they'd been called out to bring anyone in.

Wincing at the effort, Kiddo angled back on his painfully twisted arms and shoulders, drew his legs to his chest, curved his spine as much as he could, and performed the least acrobatic kick-up in history.

But it did send him successfully crashing into the Huntress.

"Houh," she wheezed, the wind being knocked explosively out of both of them as Kiddo went down yet again.

Yet, less successfully, the Huntress swung the gun wide toward the back wall as she collapsed. She tightened her grip instinctively.

And there – it turned out the gun really was the worse threat after all. Creating enough noise to bring down the house.

Unlike in the movies, Kiddo didn't have time to register what had happened until it was over.

Laine had been cowering between Kiddo and Seethe one moment, then in front of Seethe the next.

She didn't have time to yell a Hollywood 'nooo' as the shot was fired.

She probably didn't even have time to think.

She just jumped up when the gun swung Seethe's way.

She could have blinked and the bullet would have flown right over her head and into Seethe's stomach. But instead, it was now in her chest.

It was the quietest and most still that Kiddo had seen her. No wailing, no sobbing or helpless nerves.

She simply turned to the shocked, straining, devastated Seethe, and she put her arms around him.

She slumped against him and he did his best to nestle his head against hers.

Kiddo gasped as he felt the Huntress raise her weapon again, ready to try to take control of the situation.

But in an instant, strong hands had gripped her head, and she had been given an unwanted neck adjustment.

The Huntress twitched and then went still beneath Kiddo, at the same time that Laine crumpled to the floor.

Seethe was the one sobbing now, only able to stare down at the body of the first person he'd been brave enough to love.

Dom sat Kiddo up.

He had that Stanley knife again, and sliced through Kiddo's bonds.

Kiddo couldn't help groaning as his arms were finally able to swing forward.

"Go," Seethe choked. "Hurry."

"They … don't know about either of us," Kiddo told Dom, quickly stretching out his shoulders. "They were the ones on duty. Nobody else was around to see."

Dom was steely faced. He made sure the gun was obvious in the Huntress' hand. Then he placed a roll of money in Laine's hand. The same roll of money that had been in the vest pocket of the baron's ally.

There was a beating at the door.

"I'm so sorry brother," Dom wrapped an arm around Seethe's neck and pressed their foreheads together.

"Not … everything is ruined," Seethe husked brokenly. "Get out of here."

Dom nodded. He slipped his utility knife into Seethe's

back jeans pocket. He hauled Kiddo to his feet, and then boosted Kiddo up to the vent from earlier.

There was the scrabbling sound of keys from outside.

Dom propelled himself up next, using his upper body strength and following Kiddo in. He was settling the vent cover back into place as the door burst open.

Kiddo had pressed his hands to his mouth to try to keep from breathing too loudly.

He could feel his eyes bulging with the effort to be still and quiet.

"Now what in the world went on here?"

There were footsteps into the room. A number of people entering.

"*Such* a mess." The man's voice sounded totally unbothered, despite the carnage and his remarks.

"We'll clean it up Yorak," someone answered swiftly. Keen to please.

"Yes, it'll be good as new for the auction!"

The footsteps got closer to the glass office.

"Curiouser and curiouser," Yorak's voice mused. "A very odd scene indeed."

"It looks like an in-fight, Yorak. It happens."

The footsteps stopped close to where Laine and Seethe would have been.

"Tsk tsk. It should not happen to my Hunters. We are not simple snatchers anymore."

"You're right Yorak. It's an embarrassment. Probably lucky to be rid of these ones if they can't behave."

There was a suspenseful hush for a moment, as Yorak must have been surveying the scene.

A gun.

Money.

Death after a fight.

It all did go together rather well.

"Yorak," someone said uncertainly. "This one is a civilian."

Laine. In her fluffy sweater, with her tumbling curls and her sweet face. Huddled at Seethe's feet.

She was the polar opposite of the dead wolf toothed soldiers of The Hunt.

"Mmmm," Yorak replied thoughtfully. "This one is … *was* … our prisoner's dear lover," he remarked. "I spoke to her myself on the abduction night. Gave her our contact card and made some promises I wouldn't keep."

"Bastard." Seethe's voice was running hot with rage, grief and delirium.

"Oh yes, please do say your piece," Yorak said to Seethe. "What does our only witness have to share?"

Kiddo could imagine Yorak moving closer to Seethe.

"My, my, what dilated pupils you have. You are clearly quite upset," Yorak went on.

The drug baron would not have been running around telling everyone upstairs that he had a plan to drug their precious sale item into becoming a relapsed addict. Just as he would not have mentioned the roll of money he had doled out to corrupt a Hunter.

"Of course I'm upset," Seethe spat. "My girlfriend is dead

because she tried to bring you money to free me. And your thugs killed her for it."

"And each other, it would seem," Yorak decided with distaste. "But I would have erased her anyway. I didn't ask for money, I asked for Raze."

Seethe was breathing so heavily that it was audible from the chute.

"I am Raze," Seethe said in a low voice.

"And a wonderful Raze to start us off with," Yorak answered. His voice retreated, as if he was speaking over his shoulder. "But not the Raze I prize above all."

His steps halted at the door to the open room.

"We'll need a new patrol group to replace this one," Yorak stated.

"Sure, Yorak. I'll organise it at once."

"Then come back with some mops and be a good clean-up crew," Yorak told the Hunters who had come with him. "It's good character building for you to deal with the fallout of what greed can do to you in this line of work."

"Yes Yorak," there were the sounds of many feet hurrying after him.

"And you'll have to deal with the civilian's body thoroughly. She of course had a surface identity," Yorak's voice was moving further away from the room. "She needs to disappear completely."

"Yes Yorak."

"We'll take care of it Yorak."

| 21 |

Twenty One

Dom got Kiddo out of the chute system as quickly as he could, because Kiddo just couldn't chute shuffle quietly enough.

They slithered out of a vent on the second floor and scuttled around a corner, keeping flat against the wall.

Dom drew Kiddo to focus on him for a moment, pressing his lotus tattooed finger to his lips and tapping the hands-free at his ear.

Jingle and Start were in his head, telling him exactly what to do, and when.

Kiddo nodded.

Dom wrapped his hand around Kiddo's, gripping him firmly.

He was listening.

Then he squeezed Kiddo's hand, and they were off, ghosting down an aisle.

Left, straight, then fast behind a partition wall.

Two Hunters patrolled past in the distance, un-worried.

There were the faint sounds of them complaining that they'd had a last minute shift change and been called to duty.

Straight, straight, stop and duck.

Oh dear. There were Hunters blocking the stairs down to the first level. These ones were definitely unhappy to have been pulled from a break.

But not as unhappy as Kiddo and Dom were to see them there.

The first level was their way to get back to Miss Lotus' tunnels.

Dom listened again. And grimaced.

He peered over his shoulder.

Kiddo grimaced too.

A balcony? Really?

Symbolically, the heavens had begun to storm outside, as if the view from the balcony summed up what a bad idea trying to jump from it was.

Dom's eyes widened as his helpers told him something else. Kiddo followed his gaze.

Another group of Hunters was moving towards them casually. Chatting, stepping around built in desks without checking them closely, but approaching nonetheless.

Perhaps Yorak had been displeased enough after the 'in fight' mess to tighten up the ship and circulate more Hunters. Maybe they were checking for anything suspicious. Like two young men crouching in a corner.

Or perhaps they were headed to the balcony themselves. Kiddo noticed one of the approaching Hunters held a pack of cigarettes.

It would be impossible to miss the two of them if they passed that way.

Then there was a terrible screeching outside, as if a car was doing an epic burnout, before a horrific crash. And the power went out in their building.

"Aw shit!" one of the approaching Hunters stopped and cursed, peering out a window. "Someone just crashed into the power pole out there. A line's down."

"Yorak's gonna be unhappy if there's no electricity for the guests!"

"I'll organise a generator, you get onto the power company, and you keep the authorities outta here."

They swerved from their path to the balcony and headed to the stairwell.

"You lot stay on duty. Watch the stairs," they told the other group beyond the room.

Dom tugged Kiddo to army crawl quietly across the nice office carpet with him.

They zig-zagged down low, keeping under the cover of fancy floating desks, until they reached the glass door to the balcony.

It was raining outside. Heavily. From those symbolically foreboding heavens. And the wet blew in over their bodies as soon as Kiddo started inching the door open.

He gritted his teeth. Better to do it quickly and quietly than to draw attention by letting too much cold air in for too long.

He slid it open, and they both slipped out into the downpour, crouching and pulling the door closed again.

"Do we have to?" Kiddo grumbled, only half jokingly.

"Sure, we've got this," Dom said certainly, huddling out of sight from the stairs inside. He wrapped the handsfree in Pash's bandana and pocketed it to try to keep it dry.

They were both already saturated to the bone.

Kiddo huffed and edged his way to the ledge, which was covered in cigarette butts, to peer over the safety railing.

"Fine, maybe we've got this," Kiddo sighed. "If we dangle straight down to reduce the distance, there's a nice nature strip below. Land on our feet and roll, and maybe we'll just bank up a few more bruises."

Dom nodded. Taking a deep breath. "Best do it while the street is focused on Velvet and Tiny's car crash."

Kiddo gaped.

"Oh, no, Jingle said they weren't actually in it. They did it to help us out. They'd been poised and waiting for her to announce the right moment."

Shaking his head, Kiddo checked that he was out of the line of sight of the guarded stairwell on the opposite side of the building.

He and Dom straddled the balcony, gripping the railing tightly.

"I love that there's the added challenge of the wet," Kiddo grunted.

"An obscuring veil to cloak our escape," Dom remarked.

And they lowered themselves over, letting their bodies hang for a moment.

"Ready…" Kiddo panted. "Go."

They released their hold, feeling their stomachs seem to defy gravity to jump up into their mouths, while everything else dropped the distance to the grass. They hit the lawn with knees bent and then quickly angled to tumble onto their sides.

They wound up puffing at each other in the wet grass for a minute – winded, scraped and buffeted, but unbroken.

There were flashing lights further up the block as emergency services puzzled over the apparent hit and run to a power pole. But otherwise, the streets were near deserted, with only a few people dashing with their heads down to get out of the rain.

"Oh if we must," Dom gasped, and struggled to his feet stiffly when Kiddo managed to straighten up first.

They jogged together for a number of blocks before Dom finally caught at Kiddo's elbow, panting and bent over.

"I'm good for … short bursts," Dom puffed. "I mean … um … we should … hide."

Kiddo squinted through the rain, and then dragged Dom over to rest on the sheltered stair to a closed shop's doorstep.

It was an out of the way spot and would be safe enough if anyone happened to peer down the street in search of Razes.

Dom sat wearily on the top step, and Kiddo collapsed on the step in front of him, leaning back against Dom tiredly.

Though he couldn't offer any physical heat, Dom leaned forward to hold Kiddo from behind, catching his breath and shivering.

They were both soaked through, their clothes clinging to their bodies and their hair dripping into their eyes. But the cool was soothing the cut on Kiddo's head, and easing the ache along his cheekbone from where the gun had struck.

"We're lucky you didn't have a fit," Dom said unhappily

after a number of minutes of just holding Kiddo back against himself.

"I haven't decided against it yet," Kiddo replied as Dom tilted Kid's head to get a look at the cut that the bullet graze had left him with.

It tingled and stung in a fierce line.

"That was close," Dom said grimly. "So close."

"I was holding the Doctor to comfort her when she pulled her surprise," Kiddo admitted nauseously. "I never saw it coming until it was right in my face."

Dom pursed his lips, clearly trying not to speak ill of the dead.

"Jingle said to tell you that Pash was ok," he told Kiddo, going for a subject change instead.

He began massaging Kiddo's neck gently with a thumb.

Kiddo felt any final tension loosen in his body, and he sank back further against Dom in relief.

"Pash's upset that her bulletproof chest looks like it has a third nipple in it though," Dom went on. "And her real chest has a mighty bruise."

Kiddo rubbed his chilled fingers over Dom's knee.

Pash and Kiddo had both been incredibly fortunate. They would have to thank every single one of Sparks' lucky stars.

"How did you know I needed you?" he asked Dom after a moment.

Dom kept lightly manipulating his neck, and Kiddo found that any remaining flashes in his vision really were starting to fade.

"I was working with Jingle and Start to move around the lower levels, putting cameras out," Dom said. "I hadn't really been at it long, before Hato commented on Trix's laptop being down. Then Quicklips sent a distress message a few streets away from the tower, and Blossom was calling Hato directly."

Kiddo followed when Dom stood, spotting a taxi cruising slowly down the road in search of rain stranded pedestrians.

Dom hailed it, and they ducked past its lifting door to slide in.

Thankfully the rain had rinsed much of the blood on Kiddo away, or had helped it to blend into his navy t-shirt. But they had no way to hide Dom's identity revealing, and not entirely acceptable ink on a subway, and they were just both too bone tired to traipse through the tunnels again.

Even through Dom's clinging shirt, Kiddo could tell that his dragons and koi fish were goosebumped with cold.

Kiddo looped an arm around Dom's shoulders and pulled him in to lean against himself.

"I left the camera I was meant to be careful with, wedged into that vent you know," Dom said quietly after a bit. "I heard the gang react when they saw you get marched into Seethe's cell."

"That wouldn't have been a fun moment for either of us then," Kiddo grimaced.

"Jingle was already using the cameras I'd stuck up for her, trying to shout clear pathways to me quickly enough to keep up with my careening," Dom admitted. "Lucky she kept her head. Because I wasn't being very smart."

"That's what teams are for."

Dom gave a half smile. "Thank my lucky stars I've got such a team," he quoted Sparks himself. "Because Start was navigating all of our other scattered team mates to safety, Velvet and Tiny were concocting a commotion, Jingle was guiding me, and Hato was distracting your group until I could get there."

Kiddo chuckled in surprise. "He called on purpose, to slow them down?"

"He went all out, I believe," Dom gave a bigger smile. "Short of flipping the table, he pulled out all of the theatrics he could."

Dom rested his head against Kiddo.

"Speaking of theatrics," Kiddo said with distaste. "Did you see the chompers on those Hunters?"

Dom snorted. "Sure, they're intimidating, but are they practical? Imagine how many times you'd bite your tongue."

"I guess it's a less obvious giveaway than the mask," Kiddo sighed. "But it doesn't hide you from the world as much as mark you out in it."

Kiddo paid for the cab as they pulled up outside the Lotus Bar, and they stepped gingerly out into the easing mist of rain.

Kiddo gazed back in question when Dom tugged him to a stop before he could enter the bar.

But, unworried by the rain or by anything else in that moment, Dom stepped close so that his shoes created an alternating pattern with Kiddo's. He wrapped his arms around Kiddo so that Kid could feel the press of Dom's hands against his back. He rested his chin on Kid's shoulder so that his face was very close to Kiddo's ear on his good side.

"Kiddo?" Dom asked.

Kiddo shivered at the warmth of Dom's breath mixing with the icy trickles of rain on his skin.

"Mmm?" Kiddo contentedly circled his arms around Dom, as if they were in a slow dance so slow that it consisted of total stillness.

"That there, with Seethe, and then with you," Dom said. "That was some of the hardest stuff I've faced."

Kiddo considered the other hard things he knew Dom had faced in his life, and pressed Dom to himself more tightly.

"But Kiddo …"

"Mmm?"

"Moments like this one here, are the best."

Kiddo smiled. "I agree."

"And Kiddo?"

"Mmm?"

Dom waited just a second. Drawing the moment out between them.

"I love you."

Kiddo leaned his head so that their temples were touching.

"And I love you too."

| 22 |

Twenty Two

"Are you two coming in, or not?" Blossom called from the side entry, leaning out to yell at them.

She threw them a towel each when they joined her in a blue lit room full of screens. On the other hand, Ryo approached more gently – bringing Kiddo into better light and dabbing at the side of his head to help him clean and dry the wound.

"That looks painful," Ryo sympathised, as Kiddo gratefully leaned against a metal desk and allowed him to assist. He even rubbed with care at Kiddo's hair for him so that it wouldn't keep dripping into the cut.

"I'm numb all over now," Kiddo answered, only half joking as he watched Dom roughly towel dry his own hair. "So it doesn't really matter."

The room's lights made Dom's lips appear even bluer than they had been outside.

"Unfortunately, I didn't get finished with the washing, after the interesting find I had this morning," Ryo said apologetically. "But I keep some spare shirts up here in case I ever need a quick change for the bar."

He crossed to a cabinet in the corner and selected two crisply pressed, neatly folded men's tops. They were plain, but elegant and comfortable, and they had blissfully long sleeves.

"You're the *best!*" Dom rewarded Ryo with one of his fast, and this time dripping hugs, along with a dashing grin, before pulling his own clinging shirt off immediately to dry and change.

Kiddo found that he wasn't even jealous anymore, and he straightened wearily to do the same thing.

"I'll add your additions from today to the load," Ryo answered wryly.

"Hey, Ryo, maybe you should get them some pants too," Blossom commented enthusiastically, watching them change with her pierced eyebrow raised.

"Stop objectifying us," Dom admonished, while totally unbothered.

"You know, you've managed to make yourself even handsomer now," Blossom ignored Dom and directed her attention to Kiddo.

Kiddo was carefully avoiding getting the fine material of Ryo's shirt near the cut on his head, and drawing it all the way down to warm his skin.

"With a scar like that you're just slightly less perfect, and more rugged," she said factually.

"Miss Lotus will help you with it," Ryo also told Kiddo, more practically. "Lucky your hair is already shorter on the sides."

"We better head down and regroup," Dom said then, and his posture drooped slightly. "Did our team come in all bedraggled and morose?" He suddenly seemed flat at the day's events himself.

Ryo clapped him on the shoulder, leading the way to the elevator. "Exhausted and worried. But not defeated."

"Say hi to Trix for me!" Blossom called after Kiddo as he closed the office door.

And, as Ryo had said, the team's spirits were not dire.

They had been invited into Miss Lotus' home so that they could all meet together while Miss Lotus tended to Kiddo's head.

He'd wound up with a makeover when she had decided she preferred to shave the side of his head. Then she'd decided that she'd better do some work all over so that he was still pretty.

The feel of the razor running over his scalp had been almost therapeutic. The antiseptic, not so much. And now that he was laying on his side with his head resting on a cushion in Miss Lotus' lap, despite the awful sensation of tugging and pricking as she stitched him up, he could only stare blearily while the group talked over him.

"Dom got a fair few cameras up when he was doing his dash around the building," Jingle was saying. "We'll be able to use that to our advantage."

"They also never reported that we were in the tunnels beneath the tower," Start added. "We could still use the plan for random entry and attacks from the first floor."

"You couldn't ship our specialty grenades into Japan in time," Flip commented. This time Sparks and Hato were both sharing his camera, and a flashy dishwasher was visible behind them. "Which means you're limited to close quarters fighting, or to terrorist scale building damage."

"There are too many of them against the few of us for close quarters to be an option," Trix stated. "And taking down a new building, as well as putting other people and buildings in the area at risk is not an option."

"I say you go to war," Miss Lotus stated calmly as she stitched. "And my followers go with you."

There was silence as the group regarded her, with growing hope now as they imagined what that could involve.

"The issue is taking root here, on *our* turf," Miss Lotus went on. "We aren't happy about it. And we want to clean up our area."

"I've noted twenty more guest arrivals for an overnight stay at the tower," Jingle said. "One even just got in by private helicopter a few minutes ago. They have catered enough food for perhaps one hundred guests and reps altogether. And I'd say there are about eighty Hunters there, with at least double that in regular snatchers who have been arriving to keep an eye on the surrounds."

"Those numbers are nothing," Miss Lotus told her. She tied off her final stitch and Kiddo felt the cold blade of a small knife against his head. His gaze was fixed ahead on Pash, who lounged directly across from Kid, rubbing at a big bruise on his chest.

"My people can fill the tunnels and pour out into the streets to take care of those snatchers roaming the outside," Miss Lotus said. "And they can be a wave of destruction spilling through that building alongside your team. Blossom and Ryo can co-ordinate with you, and with the law afterward."

"Miss Lotus' people could block escapees from leaving the building, and block back-up from entering," Velvet considered it. "We could lock down the whole street."

"The buyers and the reps on the inside won't be helpless," Hato warned. "They will be filthy rich, high class, but really just the highest of the low. Most of them will fight as fiercely as The Hunt will."

"But we can hope that, at an intimate event of powerful people, weapons won't be tolerated," Start chipped in. "Jingle mentioned that only a few of the patrol Hunters in the outer halls and stairwells seem to be obviously armed so far."

"Wouldn't want the buyers to feel threatened or trapped," Tiny rolled his eyes, clutching a thimble-like cup of steaming tea.

Miss Lotus was now dabbing something like petroleum jelly against Kiddo's scalp.

"Because Dom left a well-positioned camera over Seethe's cell, we can guess at the order of events for tomorrow," Flip announced. "They've been setting up display cases, spotlighting and a podium. It seems that there will be a number of exquisite collectables auctioned first, so that Seethe can be the grand finale."

"The good news is," Jingle added, yet in a negative voice. "With more buyers arriving, for short intervals they've let Seethe roam the small office-turned-cell, free of his bonds, so that people can get a good look at him wildly pacing. He's quite the attraction."

"He's been injected again," Hato rumbled unhappily. "The baron must have found a new Hunter to help him know when Seethe is safely strapped up and alone."

"And he didn't make a sound as they removed Laine's body," Start shuddered. "Hopefully by then the drugs had made him numb."

Miss Lotus put a hand on Kiddo's shoulder. "All done," she told him. And then she shook him gently in concern when he didn't move to sit up.

"Kid's looking fuzzy," Sparks' voice commented abruptly.

Dom leaned close and peered into Kiddo's face.

"Uh oh," Tiny grunted.

"How long's he been staring like that?" Dom asked Pash.

Quicklips dialled for Frazzle.

"Uh," Pash sat up straighter in surprise. "On and off for the last ten minutes. He was blinking a lot just before, but otherwise he's been blank. I just thought he was daydreaming."

"Did you hear that?" Quicklips asked Frazzle.

Frazzle had been caught off guard. He appeared to be out to breakfast somewhere nice with Doctor Daleeah. Frazzle had ironed his shirt, and Daleeah's hijab had diamante patterns on it.

"He's normally all jerky during a seizure," Flip commented. "Why's he so still?"

"What's going on?" Hato asked. "Is he alright?"

"A seizure?" Miss Lotus asked Dom. She said something in Japanese.

"He has epilepsy," Dom explained. "But it has been so well controlled lately."

"Calm, calm, it's ok," Frazzle interjected from Quicklips' phone.

"Where he is lying right now, surrounded in cushions and on his side, is perfect," Daleeah said reassuringly. "It's an absence seizure, or it's a few in a row. It will pass."

"He can stay right where he is," Miss Lotus said, cupping Kiddo's cheek. "I don't mind."

But Kiddo blinked at Dom after a moment, surprised to find them all watching him.

"Sorry," he frowned. "Must have phased out. Bad attention span."

Dom released a pent up breath.

Miss Lotus patted him on his back and he remembered where he was.

"Oh, wow, sorry Miss Lotus," he said again, bashful to still be laying on her, and he shifted to sit up while rubbing his eyes.

"It's alright," Daleeah announced. "It happens sometimes. He was nearly shot in the *face* earlier, and had quite the exhausting day."

"Rest and recover," Frazzle agreed.

"Well, that's settled," Dom answered. He stooped to take Kiddo's hand and draw him up. "Doctor's orders. Good night," he told the others, leaving for the cottage.

And Kiddo did sleep deeply from the comfort of their bed for a while.

It was simulated night outside their cottage, and his stomach was telling him that it was upset at having missed lunch and dinner when he woke.

However the thing that had gradually led him to surface to wakefulness had been a growing awareness of someone's fingertips, gently massaging up from his collarbones. Along his neck. Focusing on the pulse point under his jaw. And then more firmly behind his left earlobe.

Dom smiled indolently when he saw Kiddo was awake. He was leaning up on an elbow on his side, and he didn't pause his rubbing.

"I love when you decide I could do with your massages," Kiddo stretched.

"Vagus nerve stimulation," Dom corrected. "And a focus on the carotid sinus in your neck."

He leaned forward with a devilish gleam in his eyes. "The vagus nerve can be stimulated from sensory spots in your ears too, you know." He bit lightly on Kiddo's left earlobe, and tugged it downward.

Kid froze mid-stretch and his eyes closed again of their own accord, but not from tiredness this time.

"You are very clever," Kiddo uttered, in bliss as Dom's lips instead of his fingers moved to Kid's neck and collarbone. "Thank you."

Dom pressed against him. Skin on skin. Moving those lips down to Kiddo's chest.

"You are …" Dom said between kisses.

Then Dom started kissing a trail downward.

"… very welcome," he breathed against Kid's naval.

They really hadn't had a chance to catch up fully since they'd first got to Japan and 'consummated' the official rela-tionship …

"In fact," Dom went on languidly.

A lotus tattooed finger hooked under the elastic of Kiddo's boxer briefs.

"Your wish is my comm–"

Dom broke off at a very loud interruption from Kiddo's rumbling stomach.

"Do … do you wish for a burger or something?" Dom laughed, pulling back to stare as Kiddo groaned.

"What a way to kill the mood," Kiddo complained, before his stomach complained again, even louder.

"Dear lord, that sounds serious," Dom teased.

Kiddo sighed and sat up. "It just might be. I'm starving."

Dom tutted, and slipped out of bed. "You'll wake up the whole den if you carry on like that." He pulled on his jeans and Ryo's shirt again. "Come on, I haven't shown you the behind the scenes of Lotus Bar's kitchens. You'll love it."

Kiddo groaned again. Throwing on his jeans and cooling his jets.

His stomach said something along the lines of a surly, entitled thank you.

"Maybe you could have some fun with their giant flame grills and peek through how a Japanese kitchen is set up," Dom told him as they left the den quietly.

The lights in the tunnels back up to the bar were dimmed for night time too, and they were largely deserted at that hour, with just the guards in red uniforms to watch them pass.

"Best not risk burning down the establishment of our greatest ally right when we need her most," Kiddo yawned. "I'll stick with a regular cold sandwich instead of a burger."

They climbed a ladder up to one of the dark bar corridors.

"Your new image is pretty tuff," Dom said admiringly, tugging Kiddo closer.

"I probably look like a prisoner." Kiddo rubbed the bristly top of the new buzz cut. Though he didn't really care.

He walked with his other hand slipped into one of Dom's back jeans pockets.

"I like it. It's edgy," Dom affirmed.

They emerged from behind the ever full and ever fake washing cart.

And Dom was just about to speak again as they stepped out into the silent bar, when he froze, and Kiddo quickly pulled him backward by his pants pocket.

"Wowee," Dom mouthed after a moment. His eyes crinkled.

They'd just walked in on Trix, seated on a bar stool, pulling Blossom closer by her black lace choker. Blossom had leaned forward, her arms on either side of Trix as she'd gripped the counter.

They were positively devouring each other with their eyes, and Kiddo was grateful that his stomach didn't protest about the lack of devouring it was doing at that moment, and give them away.

"Oooooeeee. Blossom must really like Trix," Dom breathed, fanning himself as they back tracked. "She'd lined them up with a row of her specialty seduction drinks. Blossom's Hot Shots. They taste amazing. And they get ya every time."

Kiddo moved past the fact that Dom must have an intimate knowledge of Blossom's seduction methods for a reason.

She was in there with Trix, and Kid was the one Dom was grinning at.

He crept with Dom to the kitchen by an alternate door and, together, they cracked open one of the large fridges to happily carry out a raid.

| 23 |

Twenty Three

Snatchers-turned-waiters circulated with silver food platters and trays with champagne. Their material balaclavas with the bleeding fang designs across the mouths were oddly matched with formal clothing.

Guests chatted over soft music.

And Seethe was pacing in his cell like a caged lion so that all the gathering buyers could see his magnificence.

They seemed fascinated by the animal fury boiling beneath the surface of this man. This Raze.

One lady fanned herself and one man rubbed his moustache thoughtfully as they commented on the fire that seemed to rage in Seethe, and how much they would pay to use that fire or put it out.

The drug baron kept quiet and separate from the others, but also close to Seethe's glass wall. Possessively close.

He'd reportedly had a number of private audiences with Seethe now, with his new Hunter ally apparently being very helpful.

"They aren't as opulently dressed as the buyers at the expo

were," Dom whispered. "But apparently the sale of one Raze is still quite the fancy affair."

"I find it so odd that they still gather in a physical location at all," Kiddo replied, unimpressed by the finery of those in the room.

Dom pulled a face. "They like to see what they're buying. And they also like to be seen to do the buying. It's a prestige thing. Plus, the snatchers can't find anyone good enough to block Jingle from tracing longer online events back to the participants."

Dom and Kiddo's heads were close together as they took in the scene. The sound coming from Dom's phone was turned right down, even though they shared a set of earbuds to listen in from their broom closet on the first floor.

They were a tangle of limbs in the dark, with just their faces lit by the footage playing from one window on Dom's screen, and an open chat on another window. It was a new group chat, which had expanded exponentially with an influx of Miss Lotus' people, all waiting for Start's word to move.

Right then, Ryo's people were following Start's direction. According to the orders streaming on the chat, some would be spreading out below the surrounding streets in the tunnels. Others would be fanning out to take casual positions up top – subtly sealing off roads, herding out wandering civilians, or getting eyes on patrolling snatchers. They would be quietly beginning to cut down stationary snatchers around the perimeter of the tower itself, to replace them.

Already they would be holding fast, muted surprise fights through the streets, so that when the real movement started inside, they could hold the building.

At the same time, Blossom's internal team and the other Raze members were slowly coming up from the tunnels below. One by one, they had been following Jingle's guidance to crawl about the building at opportune moments, getting into hidey holes they could burst from when the time was right.

It had been slow going.

Nearly all in position, Start's update read in the chat. *Buyers also gathering. Auction beginning soon.*

The buyers did seem to be all pouring into the main area now. They were a mix of overly superior or just outright mean looking individuals, and they each stuck to their own kind. In turn, the members of The Hunt who were there to show their strength and make a good impression were a unified front, all dutifully waiting for their master to arrive.

As if their master's arrival was actually something deserving of a fanfare, the Hunters straightened, the room quietened and all eyes turned to the main door when it opened at last.

Hands behind his back in a completely composed posture, with strong shoulders, a straight, tapered back, and face arranged into a mask of polite welcome, something about this calmly quiet figure made the crowd instinctively pull back. They parted to clear his way to the podium.

"That one's Yorak?" Kiddo whispered. He hadn't been able to see when he'd been stowed up in the chute. "I didn't expect him to be so…"

"Intense?" Dom supplied. "Magnetic?"

"No…"

"Broody? Serious?"

"Attractive."

"Sure, sure. In an evil way."

"Oh definitely, that's a given," Kiddo snickered. "He's probably around your age."

"Mmm. Got to rise young in snatcher ranks. And they're often short lived positions."

"His eyes are …"

"Chilling? Devilish?"

"Different colours."

"Yep. Gorgeous."

Yorak climbed the elevated stage and came to a stop at his podium.

He gave his greetings coolly. Charmingly.

The very mixed room of disunified buyers, disciplined Hunters and attentive serving snatchers all suddenly seemed similar in how intrigued they were by the presence of this man. As if he radiated some kind of gripping power.

"I've read about dictators who had influence like this," Dom commented darkly. Even worriedly. "The power to make people listen."

Kiddo noticed that Yorak's teeth were perfectly straight. Not filed. He hadn't had to be branded as part of The Hunt he led.

"I wish to take this opportunity to open with an acknowledgement and a reassurance," Yorak was saying. "I wish to acknowledge the beauty of the snatcher system that has existed, and all that it has given to us."

"Interesting opening," Kiddo frowned.

"… When the snatchers find a youth lost in the chaos, we change the course of their lives. We keep those we can shape, those inclined to follow, and we give them order, self-respect and opportunity."

While Kiddo was frowning, Dom's eyebrows were so high as he scoffed that they were threatening to leave his forehead.

"And while snatcher training involves great pain, repetition and rigour, it also is balanced with great reward," Yorak said smoothly. "We give the most successfully conditioned and deserving of these lost youths a place of belonging, as snatchers themselves."

"Deluded," Dom was muttering. "Absolutely deluded."

"But hope is not lost for those we sell on, who have enough spunk, health or useful attributes to be suited for the needs of our buyers. Instead, these youth are given work and get to have purpose to their lives, even if in sacrifice, when they otherwise would have been without use. And you, our buyers, are supporting those purposeless souls in their need."

Remember, Start was typing. *Fast and efficient. Corridor attackers are to move up level by level and secure the passages. The group headed to the auction room are to push right through – do not engage until you reach the third floor...*

"Now, a moment of reassurance," Yorak continued. "Out of the snatchers' recent challenges, The Hunt has been born. We are here to protect you, our buyers, and the snatcher way of life from the terrorism and anarchy wrought by the Raze gang."

There was relieved applause.

"Oh you just *wait,*" Dom growled.

"But perhaps more importantly, I have been chosen to lead the snatchers and The Hunt in a war on Razes."

Beyond a few sips of champagne, the crowd didn't stir. Listening avidly.

"He just said his war is more important than their safety, and they swallowed it," Kiddo gaped.

"Yet we do not aim to simply kill the Raze gang or their recruits. Wastefulness is not the way of our system," Yorak told them. "Instead, we will twist them into supporting our system. We will make them useful – rare collectables to capitalise on. And, as a Raze symbolises rebellion and chaos; to *possess* a Raze, or even to a lesser extent a recruit, will in turn be a symbol of the buyer's power to assert control. From tonight, a Raze will be the most prestigious item any person on Earth can own. The higher ranking the Raze you buy is, will be a reflection of your own power. And every time a Raze makes a hit on a snatcher, or even manages to sabotage a whole base, that Raze simply goes up in value. As they become more dangerous against us, and more skilled, they will become more precious. More desirable."

"Gross," Dom scowled.

"In fact, if they were to attack us here, right now, tonight," Yorak said with a deadly straight expression. "It would simply make us want them even more."

"Uh …" Kiddo was frowning again. "Let's hope he doesn't have psychic powers."

Start: rea•y ... count•own to begin.

There was some sporadic clapping as Yorak paused.

"I think he genuinely means it. He enjoys this new role,"

Dom shook his head. "Well then, he'll just love what we have coming up."

"So while we are surrounded in fine items to bid on," Yorak gestured to a masked snatcher, wheeling out the first lit up display case. It had a gleaming samurai sword inside. "Enjoy the sight of our final, most priceless item for tonight."

He then gestured at the main event, and people glanced back at Seethe appreciatively as Yorak continued.

"He is the first Raze we have on auction, and he will not be the last. But he is part of the inner circle of the original Raze, and as such, reflects incredible power for his top bidder."

Dom's screen was filled then with a twenty second countdown.

Kiddo and Dom disentangled themselves and stood.

"Just run," Dom reminded him. "No stopping in the halls. Let the hall monitors deal with anything there."

Ten seconds.

"I know."

"Head straight for Seethe's cell. Find a way through the glass. I'll cover you."

"Yup."

Five seconds.

"And be careful."

Kiddo grinned, and pulled Dom in by his shirtfront for a quick kiss.

And then they burst out onto the first floor.

There were the sounds of a flurry of others, thumping, dropping, springing free from their hiding spots.

The sounds of surprise and scrabbled defence. The sounds of attack. And the sounds of running feet.

| 24 |

Twenty Four

Shouts echoed down the halls.

Miss Lotus' people were a mixed, rag-tag bunch – but they were feisty.

Bloodthirsty.

They were tearing down anyone on the stairs who got in the way of the charge on the auction room.

Plain clothes versus uniforms.

They used knuckle dusters and knives. Mini katanas. A few had throwing star darts – slashing out at arteries, or being thrown with frightening skill.

The charge for the auction room did not falter as their comrades of the halls took down their opponents. Speed and surprise were the best defence against armed patrollers who had simply never seen an attack coming from under darkened desks, out of apparently empty offices and from supposed broom or storage closets.

Dom ducked under swinging arms while Kiddo skirted and bounded over squirming forms.

More and more of the hallway battlers petered off around

them to deal with these fights, but the Raze gang and the others sent on the auction room charge kept sprinting.

They could not give the snatchers and Hunters enough warning to lock the doors or organise.

Trix yowled ahead of them, barging into the main room first with Quicklips.

She sprang straight onto the back of a shrieking aristocrat while Quicklips bowled over three tough, but off guard gangsters.

Miss Lotus' followers dealt with the Hunters by swamping them with sheer numbers.

Tiny was clubbing snatchers as if he was in a baseball try out.

Pash was all knives.

Velvet was all fists.

And Dom was straight for the glass samurai case, shoving it off its trolley to smash it open.

"Where's the cell key?" Kiddo shouted into the face of a snatcher, whipping the guy around by his collar. But he just slumped against Kiddo, cross-eyed.

Kid dropped that one and tried a Hunter instead. She was trying to literally claw her way across the floor, away from Miss Lotus' people, who seemed frighteningly ravenous and vengeful.

"The cell key?" Kiddo growled, hauling her up by the back of her vest.

She coughed up blood instead of an answer, and he dropped her in disgust.

He caught a fist before it hit him in his newly stitched head, reflexively decking that person so hard in the face that they dropped, cold. Then he cursed. Asking anyone for a key in this mess was a waste of time.

"I need this for a second," he stopped a Japanese girl in her mad dash past him, and slipped one of the many throwing stars from her belt. She hardly paused, racing toward a group of snatchers trying to battle their way to the doors.

It was possible that the snatchers just wanted to get free, or that they were obediently clearing the way for The Hunt members. Which, if he had time, Kiddo would have been impressed over. He'd never heard of snatchers being so un-selfishly loyal.

The Hunters had reacted most efficiently, and were struggling to pull together a human shield for a patiently waiting Yorak.

Kiddo skidded to a stop at the thick glass wall dividing him from Seethe.

"I'm coming, I'm coming," he told the wild-eyed Seethe, who was beating his hands against the glass in rage and would of course not be able to hear Kid over the fray.

Dom was close, as promised. He was just a blur of a sweeping samurai sword, cutting his way through people to get to Kiddo. And to get to the drug baron, who would be the most likely to try to stop Kiddo.

The baron was doing well in the fight so far. He had not hesitated to step up to defend his life, as outnumbered as he was. But there would not be much he could do against Dom and his samurai.

Kiddo wedged his borrowed throwing star into the lock on the door. Then he grabbed a fallen silver platter, checking that it was thick and sturdy.

He lined the tray up, drawing it back.

Then Kiddo whacked the tray against the star so hard that one point sank through the silver, the door shuddered, the glass around the lock cracked, and the lock itself broke inward.

Kiddo only had time to watch as Seethe exploded from his cell like a tornado, mindlessly pushing past Kiddo so that Kid whirled around with the force and nearly fell into the cell himself.

Seethe, now gripping Dom's Stanley knife, and out of his mind with grief, drugs and a need to punish, cut out at masked snatchers even as they fought the Lotus and Raze gang. The snatchers whirled, clutching and screaming at the shocking tears such a small, brutal blade could make.

Within moments Seethe was a crazed demon, covered in blood. It stained his arms like gory gloves, and was smeared across his face. He did not slow, instead gaining intensity as his blade ripped and shredded a pathway of carnage toward where Dom was dressing down the drug baron.

It was as if Dom was performing a degradation ceremony for the most disgraced serviceman to have ever been dishonourably discharged. But rather than shreds of uniform being removed…

"Bleh," Kid winced at the sight getting even worse, with Seethe jumping in to take over. Shivving away with frantic, violent abandon.

How valuable Seethe and the Razes would be now.

That fleeting thought made Kiddo's eyes flick back to the podium, around the room and to the door.

In time to see Yorak, exiting amidst a now organised rush of Hunters.

Kiddo took off immediately, skidding out to the corridors to join where Blossom and her battered, but still enlivened hallway army scuffled desperately with the Hunters covering Yorak's ascent up the stairs.

"Jingle said there's a helicopter up there," Kiddo called breathlessly to Blossom in warning.

Kiddo clobbered one guy who had grabbed a handful of Blossom's hair, and she stabbed a girl who was in turn launching for Kiddo's back.

More Hunters thundered down from upstairs to barricade the way as Yorak and a smaller group kept going.

"This is useless," Blossom spat, blood on her teeth. "An up-ward battle. We've got the numbers, but it'll take too long."

Kiddo body slammed a snatcher, with a noisy rush of air and the meaty-grindy clunk of a person hitting stairs.

"Not useless," he panted, pointing at an air vent in the roof above their heads. "We don't have to be silent like Dom over this racket. We just have to go up enough to get past this blockade. Hopefully your people won't be far behind us."

Kiddo grabbed a wrist when he saw a flip switch arcing toward him, and rammed the person's knuckles into a wall.

The attacker dropped the blade with a clatter, and Kid scooped it up, making quick, purposeful slashes through barely resisting flesh and muscle.

This thing cut like a dream. Flip would love it.

Blossom eyed the vent, calculating, as Kiddo then hur-riedly gutted someone gunning for her.

"Alright. Give me a boost," she decided.

Kiddo closed the switch, pocketing it, and hoisted her up. He tried not to let her get jostled by the pushing and squirming of bodies around them.

When she was up, he spring-boarded himself off a hunched over Hunter, with Kid getting just the right amount of lift, and the Hunter faceplanting with the floor.

Swearing and sweating, he pulled himself up and in after Blossom.

"I guess I follow the incline," she said, as she started to wriggle her way forward.

"I think just a couple of vents worth of crawling should cover it to bypass the blockade," Kid grunted. "Not that running up flights of stairs will be fun, but ... faster," he puffed on some dust and wiped the sweat from his eyes.

"Why haven't they connected up their elevators?" Blossom ground the words out through gritted teeth. "Stairs suck. Chutes suck."

"No one's meant to be using the building yet. It wouldn't have been a worry."

"Gahhh."

When the noises of battle did not sound like they were directly beneath them anymore, Blossom kicked out a vent cover and they both dropped down as well as they could onto the uneven stairs.

Not waiting to catch their breaths, they kept moving at once, bolting up the stairwell two steps at a time.

Yorak's progress had been slowed by the human shield that had been surrounding him, and the battle that the Hunters had had to force their way through. But the group were still dangerously ahead.

Blossom and Kiddo both heard the whirring of a helicopter's engines getting started on the rooftop.

They pushed even harder.

"They'll need … five minutes … to warm … it up," Blossom managed.

"Justprevent –" Kiddo tried to rush the words out. "Yorakfromleaving –" step, step, step, "untilhelpcomes."

Blossom reached the rooftop entrance first, and threw herself at the door rather than testing to see if it had been jammed. The heavy door banged open, and she collided with two Hunters who had been left there to guard it, going down in a blur of punches.

The dark sky reflected Ryo's battle below too – the flashing lights of bullets and orange glow of flares illuminating the night.

Kiddo dashed onward, eyes trained on the suited man calmly walking away from him, toward the charging helicopter, as if the world around and in the tower hadn't suddenly turned to fireworks and blood.

As if he simply had to jet off to his next business engagement.

The six Hunters on either side of Yorak, and Yorak himself, had not heard Kiddo and Blossom's noisy entrance over the whirring of the chopper blades starting up. And they cried out in shock when Kiddo sprinted by them to spear tackle their leader so that Yorak went crashing off course.

Yorak reflexively twisted to grip Kiddo's shoulders while Kiddo locked onto Yorak's waist, and they both careened together – struggling all the while, off the path and into the luxurious, blue-lit rooftop pool.

The shock of the water crashing up into their noses and mouths made them both instinctively let go of each other, gaping and thrashing at their accidental intake of chlorine instead of air.

Gagging, Kiddo hardly had time to straighten before two Hunters were scraping him back over the pool's edge, hauling him up by his armpits.

Eyes, throat and stitched head stinging, Kiddo grunted as they pinned his arms and clobbered him against the wet poolside.

Kiddo kicked and arched – kneeing one of them in the jaw so hard that the man toppled backward, and then roared and dove, ramming an elbow into Kiddo's stomach so that he saw stars.

There was a bang nearby that made Kid stop writhing for a moment, instead grinding his head desperately against the concrete to peer around with dread.

It had been a shot.

A sharp crack that had been loud enough to cut across the cyclical whirring of the chopper blades.

"If that was a Raze member," a cold voice came from beside Kiddo, "it best not have been a fatal shot."

Yorak had pulled himself up to sit on the edge of the pool. Even wet, he was as smooth as ever, rather than bedraggled.

Kid wheezed and fought frantically, trying to get free despite a thick forearm that was now digging into his oesophagus.

There was a yelp as Blossom was slammed bodily against the ground on his other side, to be pinned too.

Kiddo squirmed to see her, and found that, though she

had taken down the door guards, Yorak's spare Hunters had got the better of her with a gunshot hole now bleeding from her right hip.

"Put pressure on that," Yorak ordered flatly, and then cursed, shaking his head. "She might wind up needing a hip replacement. So let's hope she's Lotus instead of Raze."

Yorak swivelled on the pool's edge to regard Kiddo then.

One eye so dark as to be nearly black, one icy blue.

"Ease off a little, he's about to pass out," Yorak commented, and Kiddo rasped for a breath of air when the forearm did stop pressing down quite so aggressively.

"The helicopter is ready, Yorak," a Huntress approached to tell him.

"You go ahead and jump in. Be ready to take off." He loosened his black tie and top button, raking his wet hair back.

There were the growing sounds of a fight coming from the stairwell, just audible over the chopper. The Raze and Lotus numbers were overwhelming the Hunters at last. Yet Yorak didn't seem overly concerned.

"You … knew this scale of attack might happen," Kiddo managed to gasp.

Yorak lifted one leg out of the water so that he could angle himself toward Kiddo politely. He leaned his hands on his knee, gazing at Kiddo, as if they were having a catch up chat by the poolside.

"I'd hoped," Yorak nodded. "It helps my long game."

"How'd … you know?" Kiddo dragged the words out.

Kid wriggled in agitation, as if he was struggling with his hands against the concrete.

"When an interesting drug baron realised he needed a

new helper, and tried to go right to the top and bribe me, I noticed that I'd seen a similar roll of money earlier," Yorak explained thoughtfully. "It made me suspicious that the in-fight hadn't been exactly as it had appeared. I was optimistic that it signalled more to come from the Raze gang."

Yorak unlaced his dress shoe and tipped water from it.

"If not, tonight's auction still would have been a great success. The baron had similar goals to mine, so I empathised and helped him out with access to your friend. He would have been a keen buyer."

Kiddo hissed, glaring hatred. He bunched his fists against the wet ground. So close to his pocket, which was thankfully still weighted down by –

Yorak lifted his other leg from the water, unlacing that shoe too.

Kiddo edged his fingers into his pocket.

Closing his hand around the switch.

Trying to be imperceptible and fast, Kiddo moved again so that it simply appeared he was angrily clenching two fists on either side of himself once more.

Yorak stood, disregarding his shoes now completely, as if shoes were not important for a suave appearance. And really, on him, it hardly mattered.

He straightened his collar.

"Lift this one up," Yorak said. "So I can get a better look without you all crushing him."

Kiddo was dragged upward, and his chest heaved for more air now that all of the weight had been taken from it.

The Hunters were wrenching his arms backward, gripping him by the biceps. He kept his switch clenched carefully in a fist.

A few Hunters were now standing at the rooftop entrance, shooting down the stairwell to prevent the horde from getting higher.

Yorak stepped closer to Kiddo, who lifted his head defiantly and glowered.

"Yes, I'm certain you, at least, are one of them," Yorak said. "You had the foresight to come here rather than just keep battling away with the masses."

Yorak lifted a hand to Kiddo's face, and ran a thumb over the aching bruising on Kid's cheekbone. The gesture was as if they had known each other for years and had no boundaries between them at all.

Since the Huntress' strike with the butt of the gun the day before, the bruising had only been added to. But as his thumb passed over the mark, Yorak's light tracing brought fleeting aches of pain to the surface of Kid's skin that might have been borderline pleasurable and teasing if the touch had been Dom's.

Kiddo refused to look away submissively. And in any case it was hard not to be caught staring into the contrast of this man's eyes – one so pale, one so dark – as he studied Kiddo so intently and unhurriedly.

"I'm something of a fan of your kind," Yorak went on after a lingering moment. "You are our exact opposites. But like the drug baron, for my own reasons, I have my sights set on one ... or now maybe *two* Razes in particular."

Kiddo sneered. "Nope, you got it in one. I'm the original."

Yorak smiled faintly. "You're all wet. I can see right through that shirt. And while you are quite the picture, there's not one tattoo in sight. I know to look out for that at least." He tilted to make eye contact with Kiddo's guards. "Bring him along."

As they forced Kiddo to follow toward the helicopter, Blossom tried to struggle, and cried out as her captors forced her back hard.

They did not expect, however, that she would be quick enough, or still strong enough, to yank the gun from the belt of the man staunching her wound.

She brandished it in their faces so that they hurriedly scrambled out of the way, flinching as if burnt. But then Blossom rolled with a scream of pain, leaning up like a commando rising to shoot. She hit two of the Hunters taking shots down the staircase from the door, forcing the others there to duck and cease fire momentarily before her own Hunters were diving back on her.

It was enough. She'd cleared the way for help to come.

Yorak sighed. He took the gun from one of his Hunters' holsters and flicked the safety off.

"Pass him to me." He waved his fingers at Kiddo, as if he were asking for someone to pass a beloved pet over for a cuddle.

Indeed, he slotted in close behind Kiddo as if holding him in an embrace. An embrace like Dom would give. Then he continued to support Kiddo against himself to keep Kid from tripping as they stepped backward together.

Apart from being used as a shield, and apart from the gun

buried in Kiddo's side – yet again, much too close for comfort – Kiddo would have felt nicely cocooned by Yorak's hold.

"I hate guns," Yorak told Kiddo. "I honestly hope no inner circle Razes have been overly damaged."

The horde started to swarm onto the roof. People burst from the stairwell, throwing themselves at any Hunters who were left.

But Seethe and Dom, tearing up onto the rooftop at the forefront of the crowd, froze when they saw Kiddo and Yorak nearing the helicopter ahead.

"Then is this just a formality?" Kiddo ground his teeth as Yorak made sure his own gun was very obviously visible; angled up against Kid's ribs, towards his heart.

"Don't test it," Yorak warned gently. "I've only just found you, and would hate to lose you." If Yorak had leaned down a little, he would have been resting his chin on Kiddo's shoulder.

"Would you stop holding him like that?!" Dom demanded hotly, yelling at Yorak as if he were more offended by the tenderness rather than by the gun that Yorak was directing Kiddo's way.

"Is that *him*?" Yorak asked against Kiddo's ear, his fascinated voice half snatched away by the wind and noise of the helicopter at their backs. "So beautiful and jealous. And you are important to him." He shook his head against Kiddo's temple and laughed in delight. "Perfection."

Dom's blue eyes were blazing, and he couldn't help stepping forward as Kiddo was drawn further backward.

"Careful, careful," Yorak called.

It was bloody, demonic Seethe, who had before seemed so far gone from reason, who gripped Dom's arm.

Velvet and Pash were stalking along, panther-like, on Yorak and Kiddo's sides, though keeping their distance.

Quicklips and Tiny were leading any final scuffles.

Trix was crouched over Blossom.

"Guys …" Kiddo suddenly yelled out in warning. They would hardly be able to hear him. Yorak had got him right up to the helicopter door now. "He wanted this to happen, he –"

"You're right," Yorak said right up against his ear, tightening his supporting hand against Kiddo's sternum. "I wanted your photographs. To build my files."

"Got them Yorak," a Hunter called from behind them in the chopper. "We'll be able to tell who might be important from the film. It will be all the ones watching your prisoner right now."

Yorak nodded against Kiddo. He began to turn.

In that moment, as Yorak's grip on him shifted, Kiddo took a chance.

He unclenched his fist and flipped the switch blade up. He arced his arm across and behind himself, as if he were doing up his seatbelt instead of driving a knife home.

Yorak was still so very closely connected to Kiddo, that as the blade pierced his side, Kiddo felt the flat muscles of Yorak's middle tighten in pain against his back.

Miraculously, Yorak either chose or managed not to tighten his own grip on the gun's trigger. It simply dropped away from Kiddo's body as Yorak hunched slightly.

The Hunt's photographer waiting inside the helicopter cursed and leapt forward, dragging Yorak backward, away from Kiddo, so that the knife pulled free and Kiddo dove away with it. Yorak clutched his side to stanch the blood, his evaluating gaze going from Kiddo to Dom as he was hauled into the cabin.

He didn't even seem angry to have been stabbed.

And as the other Razes raced forward to Kiddo, exhausted and triumphant against all but the most crucial of the Hunters, the chopper lifted off.

| 25 |

Twenty Five

"It wasn't a fatal wound," Kiddo admitted as things wrapped up and his gang joined him, standing by the pool. "I felt it hit a rib."

"Mmm. Sucks man." Seethe had collapsed onto a pool chair, empty and wiped out. Velvet perched on the end of the chair, her hand on his leg as if he might suddenly flare up again, and run away like a berserker.

Pash was behind Seethe, smoothing his long hair soothingly. She'd tried to dab some of the blood off his face while he'd been staring, but it was too big a job. Even his bare feet could have been mistaken as wearing red socks.

"That Yorak was rather taken by you," Quicklips told Kiddo unhappily, rinsing his gory knuckles in the water.

"Not just me," Kiddo glowered. "He'd gladly take Dom and I as a package deal. And he isn't against skewing the auctions to go the way he wants. He was doing it for the drug baron."

"*That's* a memory to keep," Seethe whistled slowly between his teeth. Spaced out. "Dom dropping the baron's head at my feet."

"She alright?" Tiny asked Trix, as she left Blossom and crossed to join them. He put a thick arm around Trix, while his other hung disturbingly out of its shoulder socket.

Trix had overseen the making of a stretcher for Blossom, who was now being lowered down the stairs. Ryo was rounding up teams to collect any of the injured Lotus followers too.

"She and a few others have no choice but to go to hospital for surgery. Miss Lotus has already personally organised a team of private physicians who will tend the others below ground, and has a few discreet surgeons waiting up top," Trix told the gang wearily.

"Jingle spent the raid checking out as many of the buyers as possible," Dom commented, reading a message in their gang's chat. "She's sending the authorities all the records of the buyers' dodgy dealings that she could find, so that they can see there are no clear victims here, and can hopefully put some of the puzzle pieces together to work out their side of things. It's harder when you can't just blow all the evidence up and make it disappear."

"It'll sure be confusing to find a bunch of dead foreigners in a building not open for business yet," Quicklips commented, straightening from the pool. "Wealthy criminal foreigners, and anonymous sharp toothed soldiers, to boot."

"The fallen Lotus followers might help," Dom sighed. "They are known to be vigilantes, which is one reason Miss Lotus is respected by leadership. So their presence here will be hint enough."

"Yes, and on that note, let's get going," Trix announced. She patted Tiny's good arm. "The living have got to clear out of this tower, before the authorities have to come and make sense of it all. Miss Lotus' connections can only get them to hold off for so long."

Quicklips hefted Seethe up from the deckchair, and he flopped harmlessly – passed out.

At certain points they had to move down the stairs in single file to pick their way through the carnage. It truly was as if war had broken out and been contained within and around one building.

And when Miss Lotus' medics met the many exhausted people slipping back into the tunnels, it really became like a war bunker or emergency zone.

Faces were cringing as bones were splinted. Cuts were cleaned and bound. People were limping or sliding down to rest. There were horrible sounds as others like Tiny had to have parts of themselves manoeuvred back into place.

But there was a satisfied tone among Miss Lotus' people. They had yet again sent a distinct message of intolerance for snatcher, and now Hunter activity in Japan.

"You know, I just can't get over that *og," Dom scowled as he came up behind Kiddo and grabbed his hand when the gang was ready and moving together through the tunnels. "He was more ready to seduce than to shoot you."

"He thinks you'd make a great catch too," Kiddo shrugged. "Literally."

"Pft. Wonderful."

"Don't be stroppy," Kiddo managed a small grin. "Not shooting me wasn't the worst thing Yorak did all night."

"Oh, I feel stroppy," Dom answered, very stroppily. "Can't help it."

"You are so terrible at hiding your feelings," Kiddo teased softly. "I love it."

Dom had said those exact words to Kiddo all those days earlier, when Kiddo had first been terribly jealous of Blossom and Ryo.

That got a flicker of a smile. "Watch it. I'll pin *you* against a wall this time."

"You two are so cute," Pash told them. "I'd love to see that by the way."

"And you are so cheeky," Dom said affectionately, marginally cheered up.

"Speaking of cheeky, do you think the blood will come out of this?" Pash asked. She held up a nice watch with a material covered band.

"I doubt it," Kiddo answered skeptically. "Why'd you wear that to a fight?"

"And why's it cheeky?" Dom asked.

Pash grimaced. "I forgot I'd borrowed it."

"Borrowed?" Dom inquired.

"It's Velvet's," Pash answered.

"It's *what?*" a dangerous voice hissed from slightly further back in the tunnel.

"Ooh, got to go," Pash announced. "I think Quicklips needs help with Seethe."

The spectacular, Velvet-esque cussing that issued around them for the next few minutes only petered off when they all felt the relief of reaching a green passage lined with jewelled blossom trees.

"Maybe we really should just stay down here forever," Dom sighed to Kiddo. "Where that dog won't get us."

"Unfortunately," Kiddo answered with regret. "He's a wolf. And they hunt their prey."

Seethe was still floppy when Quicklips set him down in Miss Lotus' main room. Quicklips propped him up in his arms and tried to rouse him when Miss Lotus advised they get some steamed rice and water into his stomach, brought in by her kimono wearing maid.

It was disturbing to watch the infallible, tough as nails Seethe have to be coaxed to drowsily accept small mouthfuls from the spoon that Tiny patiently offered him.

Kiddo even noticed that Velvet's eyes were damp, albeit still glaring and tough as nails too, as she helped Pash to wipe down Seethe's arms and face properly now.

Pash was forgiven.

And Velvet was gentle as she dabbed around the bruised veins in the crook of Seethe's elbow.

Though they had been able to see the chaos unfolding in the building, Hato and the gang at home all answered immediately when Miss Lotus put the call through from her main screen.

Sparks was a blur, answering even while rolling out from under a car. Flip shouted at his trainees to shut up and play dead. Start and Jingle had dark rings under their eyes. Even Frazzle and Daleeah paused in their painting of a plaster wall so that they could see if everyone was alright.

"Seethe?" Hato asked in concern. "Is he …?"

Seethe blinked a little and squinted at the screen, before letting his head drop back against Quicklips.

"Hato," Seethe managed. "M'alright."

The tension dropped from Hato's shoulders and he rubbed at his face in relief.

"But Hato," Kiddo said uneasily. "It might be worth getting Jingle's military contacts to help us secure the base further."

"We're pretty well fortified," Flip answered confidently, before he yelled back over his shoulder. "I SAID PLAY DEAD. I SAW THAT BREATH JUST THEN JEFFREY."

Kiddo shook his head. "Everything that has happened in Japan has been part of The Hunt, or Yorak's, plan. He didn't care that it meant a tower full of buyers, snatchers and Hunters might die, he just wanted to pin point exactly which of us was the original Raze, and who might be in the inner circle." Kiddo swallowed sickly. "He described the bloodshed tonight as something like a good chance for him to build his files on us. It was a photo opportunity."

"So we have to plan for a war on the home front?" Start asked, pushing his glasses up. His brain was already ticking.

"We have to keep The Lair and garage open and training going," Hato disagreed. "It won't be long before more strangers than ever are coming in to see our resident doctors. We still need open doors to provide a safe haven for those who need it."

"Actually," Kiddo said uncomfortably. "The Hunt won't be coming at us on a large scale to kill us. They'll be subtle, and will try to collect us alive."

"Yorak, the head of The Hunt, announced that Razes are a new kind of rare and precious currency or status symbol," Dom added.

"Yes, owning one of us will be like telling the underworld

you are an absolute god," Sparks commented darkly. "We heard it over the feed."

"We'll plan some stronger measures," Start promised, "that will help us keep doing what we do, as safely as possible."

"Kiddo stabbed Yorak before he got away," Pash added on a positive note. "So that'll cool his jets for a bit."

"Good on you mate," Flip congratulated Kid, before he was distracted again. "Bloody hell Jeffrey, I'll kill you for real!"

"I'll book staggered flights to begin bringing you all home," Jingle cut in. "So Miss Lotus can have peace in her den."

Kiddo noticed a faint sadness to Miss Lotus' expression. She would be losing her Raze again.

"You'll be able to leave your teeth out all the time," Dom whispered to cheer a glare from her instead.

"Should I book Seethe and a couple of carers to come last?" Jingle asked. "Give him some time to crash?"

"No," Seethe slurred. They hadn't realised he'd still been following the conversation, but his eyes were slitted narrowly open as he peered down his nose. "I want to leave this behind. I'll be on the first plane you can get."

"You mightn't be well enough for the plane," Doctor Daleeah told him with a frown of concern. "How much exactly were you injected with in this last week?"

"It started off as once every morning and every night. But then the dose was increased to every few hours for a couple days and a night," Seethe sighed and lolled against Quicklips dejectedly. "It's enough that I'm craving a hit again now. So I guess it didn't take much to bring the addict back."

Dom growled. "I would like to chop his head off again."

Jingle was scrolling on her screen. "There's a flight first thing tomorrow morning. 8am for Narita Airport."

"I can organise some medicines that will help push back and soften the withdrawal process," Miss Lotus offered. "If your medics hold on the line with me."

Frazzle and Daleeah nodded.

"Thank you," Seethe answered. His eyes closed again. Totally unbothered that Quicklips was holding his hand in comfort.

"Dom and I will go with Seethe," Kiddo announced, sharing a glance with Dom. "I know what this is going to be like."

"Alright," Jingle nodded. "I'll book those seats now. And I'll send through the details for everyone else as I sift through more flight options."

"Wait, Jingle," Trix broke her withdrawn silence. She sat forward with resolve growing on her face. "If it is alright by Miss Lotus, I would like to stay and be here while Blossom recovers."

Miss Lotus beamed. "I've grown quite fond of you all. And would be honoured to share more time, and my apprentice, with you."

"Trix, you might even spearhead a new Raze division in Tokyo," Start plotted. "We could work with that."

Trix sucked in a breath and released it. "Let's just get my girl walking again first."

Dom nudged Kiddo. "Told you. The Hot Shots. Dead giveaway."

| **26** |

Twenty Six

Saying goodbye to Miss Lotus was bittersweet.

While Doctor Daleeah was starting to feel a little like a mother to Kiddo at home, Miss Lotus had come to feel like a grandmotherly figure – or even a fairy godmother of some kind.

"Keep in better contact this time," Ryo told Dom, dragging him in for a hug. And Kiddo felt a tiny burst of warmth over that. Dom had always kept in close contact with Kid when he left.

"We'll be back," Dom promised. "To check on Blossom and Trix. And to do the million other things I never got to do with Kiddo while we were here."

"I did want to take a bullet train past Mount Fuji," Kiddo affirmed.

"And we'll be back to see our beloved Miss Lotus," Dom said.

Dom opted to kiss Miss Lotus on her hand and then her cheek, before bowing to her gravely.

"I might not be here," she replied in her dry, withering voice. "Or I might be busy."

"Oh?" Dom asked, delighted.

She just fanned herself, as pleased as a cat with cream.

"Our master has asked me to procure a wheelchair for her," Ryo informed Dom happily. "She wishes to move about more."

"And to get back to entertaining and hosting," Miss Lotus added haughtily. "I remembered while hosting your lot that I am quite good at it."

"That is excellent news!" Dom exclaimed. "As long as you background check every single person who sets foot in your world," he warned. "Because there are wolves out there."

"Yes, and they best be careful," she answered. "They've seen what we can do."

Kiddo stole a kiss on her hand too, and she patted his cheek warmly.

"Take care of him," she whispered.

And he promised.

Twenty Seven

"I'm not going to jump out the window," Seethe sniped irritably. "You don't have to sandwich me in the middle."

"You now have a choice of whose shoulder to dribble on," Dom answered calmly, putting a bottle of water in Seethe's slightly trembling hand.

"I'm so grateful," Seethe snarled.

"As you should be," Dom approved, putting a hand to Seethe's brow to feel his temperature as well as to push his head back to relax. "If it weren't for you, I'd be finding a way to get Kiddo initiated into the mile high club over this flight."

Kiddo snickered.

"I'm after a different kind of high," Seethe said flatly. "So at least we're all suffering."

He took a sip of water, but couldn't seem to face much.

"Is the stuff Miss Lotus gave you for the trip helping?" Dom asked.

Seethe must have been feeling wretched. He had a hand on his stomach, holding in the nausea.

"I'll be able to act normal to get out of the airport back

home," Seethe said. "After that … Kid knows. It'll get worse. So much worse."

Kiddo felt ghastly on Seethe's behalf. He really wasn't sure how he would have survived being systematically exposed to his specific past addictions again, let alone going through withdrawal and cravings a second time.

"You're going to have a few rough days physically," Kiddo admitted. Not wanting to bring up the rest.

Seethe rolled his head to glare at him. "Laine was the first thing in my life that made me feel … happiness. Couple her loss with the dopamine drop, and I foresee only depression ahead."

Kiddo nodded. "You're right, it's likely. But your family will be with you. Foul moods and all."

The plane started down the runway.

Seethe grimaced. "Go back to pretending it'll only be a few days."

Kiddo grabbed them some more waters and a few bags of plain crackers from the snacks trolley when they were airborne.

"Good choice," Dom rolled up his jacket sleeves. "They're easy on the stomach."

They probably made for a funny sight – a banged up skinhead, a bony and wicked tempered lion, and a heavily inked Casanova all snacking on their little flight crackers.

They alternated between encouraging Seethe to take more water and eat his in-flight vegetables, to limping him down the aisle to the bathroom. He had one more dose of Miss Lotus' medication halfway through the trip. But he mostly just slept. And, as Dom had said, Seethe had his choice of sympathetic shoulders.

"I've definitely seen the effects of drugs," Dom whispered to Kiddo at one point, as Seethe snoozed under Kiddo's protective arm. "But I haven't seen the effects of drugs leaving someone's system. How bad does it get?"

Kiddo winced. "I was young. The parts I can remember … it was bad. It took a team to get me through it. And a team to make sure I stayed past it."

Dom nodded. "There's a bigger team now. We can do it."

"Yeah, we will. But you think he was bad natured when it was just alcohol and depression," Kiddo raised his eyebrows. "We're going to meet a whole new monster."

Seethe was scowling in his sleep.

"Anger?" Dom asked.

"Maybe. Lashing out and all. But I'm more worried it'll be like he said. A total void of happiness, and taking no pleasure in life. His grief."

Dom's eyes were sad as he regarded their sleeping friend. "I can't forgive Laine. But, she was desperate. And who knows what I might have resorted to if it was you."

"You with the samurai sword when it was Seethe was quite enough of a vengeful Dom already," Kiddo shuddered. "That one's going to haunt me."

"But that one was to avenge Seethe, Hato and every snatched kid that guy ever owned," Dom pouted. "That's such a responsibility."

Seethe stirred, shifted, and then slumped against Dom then, who took his turn to tuck Seethe under his arm protectively.

"So," Dom went on after a bit. "Miss Lotus dosed him with something that means it hasn't really started yet?"

Kiddo rubbed his eyes. "I'd guess the sleep is a mix of things to do with the trauma, Miss Lotus' pills and being underfed. The kind of thing he was being injected with generally has more distressing symptoms in the come down, which haven't started. But the physical symptoms pass quickly. He needs to sweat and thrash it out."

Dom rested his head back, and angled it to regard Kiddo. "I'm sorry that you know all of this."

"Me too. And I'm sorry I did so many things to *stay* in all of it for too long," Kiddo replied gravely. "But the gang at that time; Jingle, Flip, Hato, Tiny and Seethe, helped me to cut it all out of my life – and Seethe in particular was vehemently in favour of me abstaining from everything addictive if I could. Not only because of the ADHD and epilepsy, but because he knew that a compulsive person with an addictive personality would always latch onto something new to be comforted by and crave."

"It had happened to him," Dom sighed. "Years of drinking. Which he only just gave up with the help of his now dead therapist girlfriend."

Kiddo straightened. "We'll get him to Hato. Hato has seen him through his worst before. His tough love has helped all of us for different things."

When they landed, they stood an unsteady, groggy Seethe up while the aisles cleared.

Dom zipped Seethe into his leather jacket, and instead of looking half-starved and mean – a suspicious fiend – he looked unwell and shrunken. Just an ill man in need of help. He huddled into the jacket and hobbled between them, un-threatening, and was waved on through security.

Frazzle picked them up from the airport, giving Seethe a quick once over, before driving them home.

| 28 |

Twenty Eight

There were a few dust bunnies on the stairs up to the kitchen level of the warehouse.

A recruit had left a jacket hanging over the banister.

Nothing terrible, just a bit sloppy.

Kiddo made a mental note that he wanted to come back for those later.

First the unpacking would have to get over and done with, and that meant washing, from all of the returning Razes.

No, that wasn't first. Kiddo shook his head to himself, amused at how quickly he was back to his usual internal fluster.

More important things were first.

Hato scraped his chair back from the dining table as they stepped into the kitchen.

Dom supported Seethe to stagger into Hato's arms. And Hato enfolded them both in his bear-like embrace.

The three brothers together.

Kiddo felt someone duck under his arm to stand by his

side too, pressed firmly there, and he smiled down at Sparks with gladness.

Blue overalls, oil smudges, a questionable burn mark on one arm, dark glittering eyes and an impish smile were there for him in return.

It felt like weeks had passed.

"Nice dishwasher."

"Nice haircut."

He lifted her chin with a finger, and stooped down to press his lips to hers.

When Dom and Hato helped Seethe upstairs, with Frazzle following, Kiddo scooped Sparks up and dropped them both on the couch so that she was like a koala straddling him.

"Missed you too," she gasped with a light chuckle.

He rubbed her arms with his hands and buried his face in her shoulder, breathing her in – car fumes and all – and feeling the sharp edges of her hair against her neck.

"You have no idea," he admitted.

She rubbed the back of his rough scalp.

"Hmmm," she nuzzled kisses across his cheek. "I really do."

"When I tell you I'm about to check how your head wound is healing," Doctor Daleeah's voice interrupted them jovially, "you might not say you missed *me*."

She came around the couch and set a glass bottle of disinfectant on the coffee table.

Her plump cheeks were rounded by a smile, and her floral hijab was as bright as her eyes were in welcome of him.

"I might as well get at that burn on your arm while I'm up here," Daleeah told Sparks too.

Sparks backed off Kiddo and raised her hands. "Sorry doc, I'm so busy down there."

She blew Kiddo a kiss and scooted around the couch to escape back down to the garage.

"Be *careful* with explosives then!" Daleeah called after her firmly, and Kiddo groaned.

"Hush now," Daleeah scolded. "She's wracking her brains trying to think of new ways we can protect the base. If you'd all kept yourselves out of trouble, she wouldn't need to dabble."

"The other guys started it," Kiddo defended weakly, tilting his head as she sat beside him to check his stitches.

She tutted. "No child of mine takes the bait from bullies."

"Unless the bullies are people traffickers, and your adopted gang of oversized children are protecting other youth?" Kiddo grinned.

"So, so," she relented. "And the newest I'll be adopting – your Dom, seems quite lovely."

She had been with them for a number of months, but was enough of a newcomer not to have met Dom in person before.

"I am happy for you."

"Just as I am happy for Frazzle, in finding you."

"Hadi, hadi," she quieted him, but there was warmth in her voice as she dabbed antiseptic against his head. She and Frazzle were becoming quite close in their shared vision for treating those in need.

As what Kiddo believed an idealistic doctor should be like, she was without judgment and without bias in her willingness to treat people, and in her acceptance of each very differ-ent member of the gang.

"You should get your rest," she told him then, patting him on the shoulder. "Start has drawn up a roster for all of us to take turns picking the others up from the airport or sitting with dear Seethe."

Dear Seethe? Come to think of it, he might actually man-age to temper himself a smidgen for this woman when it was her turn to sit with him.

"I'll do that," Kiddo answered. He stretched and rose from the couch. "Thanks Doc."

"It's good you are back," Daleeah told him, standing again herself. "I was sick of feeding Duncan Jr."

Kiddo pulled a face at her as she smirked.

And he picked up a pair of Jingle's shoes, a dropped receipt and someone's towel crumpled on the bathroom floor as he made his way up to his room.

"Holiday's over huh," Dom commented, leaning in Seethe's doorway. Hato was inside with him.

"OCD-like behaviours help me cope with ADHD symp-toms," Kiddo sighed like a martyr. "Or procrastinate from what I should really be getting started on."

"What are you putting off?"

Kiddo lifted their luggage, the handles digging into his free hand.

"The washing."

Dom nodded sagely. "After our little chat, I foresaw your Kiddoisms returning in the home environment," he said. "So I asked Hato for a favour."

Kiddo lifted his eyebrows. "Oh?"

Dom smacked all of the random things out of Kiddo's arms so that they dropped noisily, and pulled him up to the next level.

There was an older male in a neat uniform, dusting down the library shelves.

"Hey man!" Dom greeted him easily. "I'm Dom. Hato told me we could find you up here and let you know the influx of return travellers has begun."

"Thank you," the older gentleman replied, stopping to give Dom his full attention. "I'll have plenty of washing to do. I'm the new live-in housekeeper, Raff."

Kiddo gaped from Raff to Dom.

"It's my first day, so I thought I'd get a feel for the place while I waited for," he paused and then clicked his fingers. "The one they call Kiddo, to talk me through the list of what he likes done daily."

"This is the one they call Kiddo," Dom pushed Kid forward brightly. "He is great at lists."

"Excellent," Raff came forward, taking a notepad and pencil from his pocket. "I'm very experienced, but I understand you might prefer things done a certain way, so I'm all ears."

"Uh," Kiddo blinked at Dom. "Is this for real?"

"Yup," Dom seemed very pleased with himself. But he checked his phone for a moment in an effort to be nonchalant. "You'll be busy with culinary training and this will take some pressure off. Even if you still feel the need to do some things, you won't see as many issues to deal with or feel them piling up on you. I should have thought of it for your final year at school."

"Are … are you aware of exactly what kind of household you are getting into?" Kiddo asked Raff.

Raff tilted his head. "I've been briefed sir, on the need-to-know information, and I am very experienced, as I said," he reassured Kiddo. "I came recommended by General Wolder after my service to him before his retirement. He has a great regard for your young security tech, Miss Jingle, and owed her a favour. I was fortunate enough to be given a new job so quickly."

"You know what," Dom told Raff after checking his phone again. "We're needed elsewhere, and it won't take you long to see what running a house full of vigilante young adults living over a nightclub can be like. You don't need a list from Kiddo. You just do what feels right."

Dom put his hands on Kiddo's shoulders and started to steer him away.

"Wait," Kiddo said as he was propelled toward the stairs again. "Just … avoid the second bedroom on the right for a few days. To be safe."

Seethe's room.

"Of course," Raff promised, in no way bothered by the warning. "I'll use my own discretion, and your warning wisely."

Dom interlocked their fingers, reaching backward as Kiddo trailed him in stunned incredulity.

"Dom …" Kiddo said at last. "Thank you."

His heart was swelling.

Dom squeezed his fingers. "Course. But wait, there's more."

Then he saw what, or who, Dom was headed for on the bedroom level.

Dom kept Kiddo's fingers interlocked with one of his hands, and caught Sparks in his free arm.

She jumped up to wrap her arms around his neck and her legs around his waist.

"You were gone so long," she crooned to him as he carried her into Kiddo's room, and Kid closed the door.

"Yes," Dom answered. "I think it's time I swap with Flip. Take my turn here yelling at poor youths called Jeffery."

He threw her down on the bed.

"Now, what did you do to your arm, and did you need us to kiss it better?"

| 29 |

Twenty Nine

The weary travellers returned, one by one.

And things got bad for Seethe while Hato and then Start tended to him.

Dom left Kiddo and Sparks asleep in bed when his turn came on that first night home. But Kiddo woke to the sounds as Dom relieved Start.

He winced. Start had been too soft and sympathetic. Seethe was in a state.

Bleary eyed, Kiddo dressed and crossed the hall to keep Dom company.

Kid closed Seethe's door and sank down to sit against it as he took in Seethe, shoving Dom in the chest and telling him to piss off.

"What?" Seethe demanded in a rage when he saw Kiddo in the doorway. "You think I'm gonna run? You couldn't stop me."

Kiddo circled his arms around his knees calmly. "I remember that sense of urgency. You're at a point where you just might run. So I'll try to stop you like you did for me."

Seethe swore and slammed his hand against a wall instead of against Dom. That was promising.

"You caught me one night before I broke my neck climbing from my window," Kiddo went on. "I'd not long been brought in, and didn't know how to swing my way from the sill to the stairs."

Hato had apparently already put a lock on the window in this room.

"Drug addled little kid," Seethe thumped into the wall and leaned his forehead against it. "Nearly died."

He was heaving for breath, sweating. His body shuddering with tremors.

"Remember when you were trying to keep me clean?" Kiddo asked. "You said that in your own life the drugs as much as the snatchers–"

Seethe sobbed. "I know, I know." He rotated against the wall. "The drugs as much as the snatchers tried to destroy me," he managed. "To enslave me."

"But…?"

"I wouldn't be a slave again."

Kiddo pointed at the metal wastebin so that Dom scooped it up in time to shove it under Seethe's nose.

Seethe grabbed it and wretched into it savagely, heaving and crying.

"You didn't want me to be a slave. And I don't want that for you," Kiddo said. "None of us do."

"I know," Seethe moaned, setting the bin down and slumping to sit on the bed, his head buried in his hands.

"I don't want to be self-destructive …" Seethe admitted. "Or to let anyone else destroy me either. But …" his bony shoulder blades bunched as he tried to gather his breath and the emotion. "Laine betrayed us. And now she's dead. My chance for happiness is dead. So what's the point?"

Dom crouched beside Seethe, and put a hand on his shoulder, but Seethe sprang up as if he'd been electrified.

"Don't touch me," he hissed.

But then he sagged.

Devastated.

"Wait," he swallowed. "I changed my mind."

Dom swept forward to let Seethe slump into his embrace, holding him tightly.

Kiddo left the door long enough to pass Seethe a glass of water from his desk. Seethe, dangling over Dom like a drunken puppet, lifted the shaky glass to drink.

When Kiddo replaced it, he returned to the door.

"Fine, fine," Seethe groaned as he watched Kiddo firmly take his seat. "You harsh bastard. Trap me in."

The fire was leaving him for now, and Dom guided him to his bed, settling him under the sheet.

"You know…" Seethe swallowed thickly. "I love you both. I love you all. I'll …" he gulped. "Be able to find happiness in that again."

"It will help," Kiddo said reassuringly.

"And hey, maybe this time I'll try a male therapist to be safe," Seethe half chuckled and half cried. His eyes were red, and a tear rolled down the side of his face as he moved restlessly.

"Oh no. Even then, that might not protect you," Dom bantered lightly. "Kiddo couldn't stay straight around me."

Seethe wiped his eyes and nose roughly. Angry at himself

for feeling so low. "Eh. I doubt I'll meet a Dom kind of therapist. A guy could help if I find one."

Dom pulled himself onto the bed to lay behind Seethe, throwing a comforting arm over him.

"Please don't push us away in the meantime," Dom said, smoothing Seethe's hair.

"No, no," Seethe drawled drowsily. "That would just lose me more people."

He sobbed again, and Dom held him tenderly.

"But don't get too openly loving either," Dom warned. "I won't recognise you."

That got a puff of air for a laugh.

"The brother that I lost," Seethe gripped Dom's arm as he fell asleep.

His face looked pained even as he dreamed.

Kiddo leaned his chin on his knees.

"You ok?" he asked Dom.

Dom sniffed. "Ahh shit," he said shakily. "I'm fine. And he will be too. Eventually."

Kiddo slipped his phone from his pocket.

Kiddo: ... the next few shifts with Seethe should be done in pairs. I'm with Dom and Seethe now.

Hato: you good?

Kiddo: fine.

Hato: ??

Kiddo: no. But, yes.

Hato: can't be easy on you. Bringing past things up.

Kiddo: you got me through it, and I thought I was a no-hoper. Seethe will get through.

Flip: Tiny and I will do the next shift. Want us in earlier?

Kiddo: no. Get some sleep. I'm good at staying awake at night.

Tiny: we'll come in first thing.

Kiddo: thanks.

Kiddo: and, Jingle, when you see this, could you look into a trusted male therapist for Seethe?

Jingle: I'm awake. I'm on it.

Kiddo: thanks guys. Night.

Hato: night Kid.

Flip: and you were never a no hoper Kid. Night man.

Tiny: night.

Jingle: night xx

Each Raze member took their turn in pairs with Seethe, and at first they each came back out, shaken and pale faced for their friend.

But eventually they stopped closing his door so securely behind themselves.

| 30 |

Thirty

"You look swell, doll," Pash told Sparks as she passed him on the steps.

She kissed his stubbled cheek, heading down to where Kiddo and Dom waited on the ground level.

"They're taking me on a date," she explained. "Like, an actual date."

"Mmm, cherries," Dom complimented the print of her skirt. "My favourite." He kissed her hand, and she looped her other through Kiddo's arm.

She wore strappy black heels, but she still hardly came up to their shoulders.

"Have fun," Flip called from the open training section of the ground level.

He threw his new switch blade, the 'Yorak Stabber' at a target, and hit the bullseye with ease.

He was happy – Dom had arranged the change over with him, and Flip would be getting to stretch his legs while leading Start's international assignments against the snatchers.

"We do have plenty to celebrate," Dom remarked content-

236

edly as he assisted Sparks up into the cruiser she'd chosen for the afternoon.

"Kiddo having started his course," Sparks listed as they climbed in on either side of her. "You working from home. Me raking in millions with all my contracts."

"Our accomplishments seem smaller compared to yours," Kiddo frowned.

"Oh no," she reassured him. "I know how hard living by an alarm clock again is for you. And I know how hard sitting still is for Dom. But you're both actually enjoying giving it a go."

Dom pulled out from the garage, past two recruits standing watch, and Kiddo craned to peer at the building being remodelled across the street.

A diner.

'Kid's Place'.

Hato was renovating it for him, as Pash had hinted at what felt an age ago.

"Thank my lucky stars," Sparks moaned as she peeked under the lid of the picnic basket of food on Kiddo's lap.

"Raff packed it," Dom told her. "I'm thinking I'll marry him."

Sparks tapped her chin thoughtfully. "No. Four would be a crowd in that regard. But he can be our adopted love child."

"He'd be the most self-sufficient child," Kiddo commented. "I had to ask him if he minded me cooking in the kitchen the other day. My life has changed dramatically."

"I love that he passes Flip a glass every time he goes near the fridge," Sparks snickered. "Or Raff tells him the juice and milk are off limits otherwise."

"I love that now I only have to think about organising my own self," Kiddo admitted. "Which is hard enough."

"Wowee, would you look at this place?" Dom whistled as he pulled into their picnic spot.

He hadn't been back to the docks since what the authorities had described as: 'an inexplicable underwater earthquake event,' which had remodelled the whole shoreline.

The old warehouses, dumped pipes and seedy piers that had covered an entire snatcher base were now replaced by a flourishing community hub.

There was a children's playground, a strip of shops and restaurants, a walkway around the water, a fishing pier, a bigger boating pier, and open grounds for picnics or fun.

Kids were dangling their legs off the fishing pier and tossing hot chips into clouds of seagulls.

"Holy shit, is that a merry-go-round?" Dom gaped as they went in search of a good spot. "Where our private pipe used to be?" he pouted at Kiddo unhappily. "The snatcher base didn't even touch that side of the water. And neither did our blast. I mean, earthquake."

"It's a far cry from everything that used to be up here and down there. And the developers never even mentioned finding anything nefarious under the foundations," Sparks said. "Because there was nothing nefarious left to find."

"Flip told me the trainees work with different Razes each night to keep patrolling," Dom commented. "It's good experience before they head overseas. He said there's more to go over when we do a proper handover, but I'm worried there's not as much to pick up on in this area anymore."

"There are some low level snatchers who try to regroup

every now and then," Sparks shrugged. "But Jingle has secretly got us dabbling with the police. We're working on toning down gang violence and general crime on the streets, as well as collaborating in more subtle take downs of the high and mighty untouchables. You'll still have your work cut out," Sparks assured him.

"And," Kiddo pulled a face. "I have a bad feeling we're going to have a Hunter problem on our doorstep sooner than we can handle."

"I have a *hunger* problem, first and foremost," Dom told them. "Let's appreciate Raff's hard work."

Kiddo and Dom spread their picnic blanket and Sparks unpacked the food.

"Aww, he even put our names on our sandwich packs," Sparks said exultantly. "So that we get our favourite fillings."

Kiddo grinned around a mouthful of sandwich when all three of them felt their phones vibrate.

"Trix says Blossom is back to work today," he told them.

"Ryo will be glad that she can stop bossing him around," Dom answered.

They vibrated again.

"Pash replied with a photo," Sparks peered over Kid's shoulder.

Seethe had joined Flip in the training compound. It was a picture of them sparring. A sign that he might be getting ready to return to life and work too.

"Our turn," Dom announced. He rolled closer to them and snapped a selfie.

When he hit send, the vibrating reply was almost instant.

Quicklips: wait!!!!

Quicklips: ...

Quicklips: Raff does food to go?! Are those packed sandwiches?

Velvet: you'll never go hungry on patrol again. Look, he even puts your name on it.

Trix: who is Raff?

Tiny: best home helper ever.

Jingle: cooks, cleans, makes Flip use a glass.

Trix: but, what's wrong with Kiddo?

Sparks rolled her eyes.

Kiddo: nothing at all.

In their selfie, Kid was squinting up at the camera with the sun in his eyes. Sparks was smiling up radiantly. And Dom was kissing Kiddo's cheek.

Nothing at all was wrong with Kiddo in that moment right there.

The phone vibrated one more time, right as Kiddo set it down on the blanket and laid his head on Dom's arm.

"Leave it," Dom said languidly, soaking up the sun.

But something made Kiddo lift it one more time to check.

And suddenly everything was wrong with Kiddo in that moment right there.

"What ...?" Kid gasped.

He sat bolt upright, making Sparks jump and drop a strawberry.

"Hey," she complained, without really being bothered. Not yet.

"What's up?" Dom asked, sitting up himself in concern.

He frowned down at the phone to see what had rattled Kid so much.

And the blood drained from his face too.

"Oh shit."

A random number had joined the chat.

The random number had sent a picture of its own.

It was a picture of many figures on a rooftop. Struggling and roiling in battle. But, drawn to the forefront of the crowd were some familiar faces. And they had been circled.

Circled in red, Trix crouched beside Blossom.

Circled in red, they led the final battles – Tiny, even with one arm dangling uselessly, and Quicklips, looking like a gladiator.

Also circled in red, Velvet and Pash stalked along the sides of the picture, eyes trained on two men whose backs were to the lens.

And lastly, circled in red, were Dom and Seethe ahead of the two men – Yorak, holding Kiddo, disturbingly intimately just as much as threateningly.

Unnamed user: ... those aren't all the Razes ... But there are some more helpful pictures in this chat.

Dom swore. He had only just posted a picture with Sparks in it. And Flip's picture had been added before that too.

Another picture was posted from the unknown number.

It was a close up, cropped copy of Dom's selfie.

Sparks had been cut out, while Kiddo and Dom's faces had become the focus. Again, circled heavily in red.

Hato: this is Laine Dean's number.

"The Hunt kept her phone," Kiddo moaned. And Yorak had put Hato's saved number to good use.

Hers was the only phone in the group that Jingle had never encrypted.

Jingle: everyone, lose the phones. Home, now.

The chat disappeared from Kiddo's screen, deleted without a trace.

Jingle would be going into damage control. Working out how far The Hunt might have been able to go.

Dom pulled Sparks up to her feet at once.

"I forgot how bloody angry I was over how that dog was holding you," Dom scowled.

Kiddo stuffed everything back into the basket.

"It wasn't just my face circled in that close up," Kiddo reminded him.

"Well my face didn't even make the cut," Sparks said without a hint of victory. "Yay."

They each unceremoniously cracked and then tossed their phones into the water at the docks.

"Home?" Kiddo asked.

"Home." Dom asserted.

And, just like that, the date and the peacefulness were over.

RECEIVE YOUR EXTRA RAZE WARFARE CHAPTER WHEN YOU SIGN UP FOR SHELLEY CASS' VIP LIST. GET YOUR BONUS HERE:

shelleycass.com/coming-soon-02

LINK TO FREE VIP READER GIFT

OTHER BOOKS BY SHELLEY CASS

The Raze Warfare Series

'A Fairy's Tale' Epic Fantasy Series:
Book One – 'The Last Larnaeradee'
Book Two – 'The Raiden'
Book Three – 'The Army for the World'

Dystopian Future:
'Awaken Dreamer'

Contemporary/Action/Fantasy/Erotica:
'Darkling'

The Sleep Sweet Series for children:
Book One – 'Little Pixie's Christmas'
Book Two – 'The case of the bored baby Ace'
Book Three – 'Mum and Me'
Book Four – 'The Cloud and the Flower'
Book Five – 'Hush'

Dear reader,
I would love to hear your feedback!
Please leave a review and feel free to visit my author Facebook page
or website (shelleycass.com).

ABOUT THE AUTHOR

I was an awkward, reserved year 8 student – totally in love with the escape and comfort offered by the novels I read. I could hear the voices of the authors' characters, I could tune out my stresses and uncertainties as I journeyed with each protagonist through their own troubles. And then one day I could hear the voices of characters who hadn't been written yet, in places that hadn't been created, and I decided to write my own worlds.

In the real world I became a high school teacher, and still face the epic battle of staying afloat in all the papers I must assess. And in the real world the magic has also sometimes been hard to find. Stress and disunity surface like cancer – making the nightly news too hard to watch on most days.

But in the real world there has also been inspiration – incredible students, loved ones, golden memories, growing up, warm hugs, big laughs and good people.

One of the greatest things achieved in my lifetime that I can remember, and that had a profound impact on me, was when Australia legalised equal marriage. I'd had this terrible sick fear that it wouldn't happen, and that I would have to face the fact that a majority of the people in my country do not want progress or equality. I would have to face the fact that some of my students and friends would not have the same rights or access to a future that I could choose to have. Teaching teens to reach for their dreams in a climate like that just seemed too hopeless. But instead, I remember sitting next to mum – happy tears streaming down her face – as something incredibly good was achieved. We proved that the majority of people appreciate love and the right to love in all forms. That love is love. Which is damn important in a world that can be so harsh.

So I wrote of the things that threaten the world, and of the big and small things that save it. I wish for a real world where the air is clean, the trees can grow without concrete borders, the darkness can be cured with the switch of a light, and the people can all have long days and happy lives.